Fear ye not therefore,
ye are of more value
than many sparrows.

–Matthew 10:31 (KJV)

MYSTERIES *of* LANCASTER COUNTY

$\mathcal{B}$IRD'S EYE VIEW

MYSTERIES *of* LANCASTER COUNTY

Shaen Layle & Nancy Mehl

Guideposts

Danbury, Connecticut

BIRD'S
EYE VIEW

To Millie Sims

I thank God for binding our hearts together.
You are more than a friend, you are family.

I love you, Mom.

Nancy

CHAPTER ONE

Martha Classen Watts took in a deep breath of crisp September air. Although she'd been reluctant to join her sister Elizabeth in purchasing a "just because" gift for their younger sister, at the moment she was glad she'd agreed. Mary was so excited and happy.

"So what do you think?" Elizabeth asked. "Did you ever imagine we'd spend our Friday night doing something like this?"

"No," Martha replied, "but Mary's wanted it for so long…."

"I have," Mary said with a grin. "I'm really grateful for the gift. And honestly surprised the two of you were willing to get inside a hot-air balloon."

Martha looked around. They weren't too high yet, but their distance from the ground still made her a little queasy. She was thrilled for Mary, but she would be relieved when they landed.

She looked over at their pilot, Norman Tatlock. He'd informed them that his friends called him Stormin' Norman. Martha wasn't too crazy about the nickname. Right now, she'd rather be riding with *Reliable Norman* or *Trustworthy Norman*. She smiled to herself. Probably not nicknames most men would want.

Norman had gone over the parts of the balloon before they took off. The big balloon itself was called the *envelope*. The basket where they were seated was a *gondola*. Then, of course, there were the burners that fueled the envelope.

Martha appreciated his attempt to educate them, but she was more interested in the safety aspects of their journey. She was grateful to see that he'd checked the wind currents before they left, doing several calculations, making certain it was safe to go up.

The Lancaster Balloon Festival was a yearly event held in Bird-in-Hand. There were races, along with lots of other events. Food trucks came in from all around to feed the crowds that showed up. Tonight, there was a bonfire and s'mores. The sisters had driven over to watch the festival last year, and Martha had, out of curiosity, found out the price of a balloon ride. It was extremely expensive, but Officer John Marks, a friend of the sisters, had talked his buddy Norman into giving them a deal. It was still a hit on the pocketbook but worth it. The sisters had been working hard at their store, Secondhand Blessings. They deserved a reward that felt special, and this certainly qualified.

As other balloons began to leave the ground around them, Martha gasped. The sky was dotted with colorful envelopes, each softly glowing and lit from within. The sight took her breath away.

When the ground crew had released the cables that held their balloon to the earth, she'd almost told them not to let go, that she'd changed her mind. But now she was glad she'd stayed. This was incredible.

"It's beautiful, isn't it?" Elizabeth asked. "I had no idea it would be this—"

"Awesome?" Mary finished for her. "Brian promised me we'd do this someday, but it never happened."

Martha put her arm around her sister. "But here you are. You made it, and you didn't need Brian." Brian was Mary's ex-husband. His infidelity had destroyed their marriage and devastated Mary, but in the six years since she had grown stronger and more independent. Martha was proud of her.

Mary nodded. "I did, thanks to both of you."

Norman pulled a cord that opened a valve and sent more propane to the burners, causing the envelope to rise higher. Although it was dusk, Martha could still see the people on the ground gathered to watch the balloons take off. Mary and Elizabeth waved at them, but Martha was busy staring at Norman. She'd noticed quite a bit of drinking at the festival. She worried that he may have imbibed. Why hadn't she asked him about that before they took off?

Elizabeth scooted closer to her on the bench-like seat inside the gondola. "Everything will be all right," she whispered. "John wouldn't have recommended Norman unless he was certain we'd be safe."

"How did you know I was thinking about that?" Martha asked.

"It wasn't hard. You're staring daggers at him."

Martha took a deep breath and let it out slowly. She smiled at Elizabeth. "I didn't mean to. Why am I such a worrywart?"

"It's because you care. You want to keep us all safe."

Martha grunted. "I guess you're right."

"Just sit back and enjoy this, Martha. We might not ever get the chance to do it again."

At Elizabeth's words, Martha settled back in her seat, determined to appreciate this unique experience. She looked around again at the other balloons. Most of the envelopes were made of brightly colored material sewn together in geometric patterns. Then there was one that looked like a big blue dog. Their own balloon was striped with vivid rainbow colors. It was certainly eye-catching.

While Elizabeth and Martha looked down at the countryside below them, Mary chatted with Norman. Finally, she sat down on the bench opposite them.

"Did you know that some balloons can seat thirty people?" she asked.

"Thirty?" Martha repeated. "You'd never get me on something like that."

"Norman says hot-air balloons are very safe. There haven't been many serious accidents."

Martha snorted. "It's not like Norman would tell you something different."

Norman pulled the cord again, and they rose even higher. Martha took another deep breath and watched her sisters, who had spotted some deer in a field below them. Elizabeth joined Mary on the other side of the gondola so they could watch them. Martha stayed where she was. Moving around made her nervous.

As they drifted farther east, they passed over Bird-in-Hand. The town looked so different from the air. People below stopped and stared at them. Some even waved. Martha finally gave in and waved back. It seemed a little silly, but after doing it a few times, she had to admit it was fun. As if they were sharing this unique experience with others.

Norman finally told them he was heading back. "I think we'll be able to land at the festival grounds," he said. "There's not enough wind to throw us off course."

Martha felt a twinge of regret to hear that their adventure was nearing its end. Elizabeth was right. This could be the only time they'd ever get to ride in a balloon. As they began to circle back, Martha continued watching the ground below them, though it was getting a little harder to see in the waning light. She could still make out houses, fields, and farm animals. They passed Rachel Fischer's house, but no one was outside. Rachel was Amish and had been a good friend to the sisters over the years, even helping out in the store when they needed assistance.

They crossed the Fischers' fields and before long passed over their own property. Mary and Elizabeth leaned over the side of the gondola so they could see their house as they floated by. Martha focused on the scenery below her, not willing to move from her spot. Lights twinkled from farmhouses nestled inside groves of trees turning autumn colors, a promise of winter on the way. Some of the fields had already been harvested. It seemed as if the land was preparing for rest. It felt so peaceful.

As they drifted toward an abandoned hardware store not far from the highway, Martha noticed a couple of cars in the parking lot with their headlights on, providing enough illumination for Martha to see a man and a woman standing in the lot facing each other. As she watched, it didn't take long to realize that something was wrong. The man grabbed the woman and began to struggle with her. Martha wasn't sure, but she thought she saw the woman look up. Was she searching for help? Then the man raised his hand, brought it down, and the woman fell to the ground. Shocked, Martha's natural reaction was to yell at the man, but she thought better of it when she realized he couldn't possibly hear her.

The man pulled the woman up from the ground and hurriedly pushed her inside one of the vehicles. Before the man got behind the wheel, Martha thought he might have glanced up too. Had he seen them? Martha quickly pulled back.

"Hey," she said loudly, trying to be heard over the sound of the burners. "Something's wrong."

Elizabeth turned around. "Did you say something?" she asked.

Martha pointed over the side of the gondola. "I think a woman is being kidnapped."

She turned back and watched as the man sped off. They were soon out of Martha's sight, the hardware store hidden behind a copse of trees. Although she'd tried hard to spot something that would help her describe the man or his car, it was nearly impossible. She hadn't been able to clearly see the woman's face either. She felt so frustrated. How could she tell the police anything that would help them rescue that poor woman?

Elizabeth and Mary scooted toward Martha and were trying to look over her side of the gondola when Norman reminded them about too much weight on one side.

"I need one of you to move toward the middle," he said, frowning. "You're throwing off the balance."

"We've got to do something," Martha said as her sisters moved away from her.

"It's getting dark," Mary said. "Are you sure you saw someone being abducted? Maybe they were just having an argument."

"Of course I'm sure," Martha snapped. "I think I know the difference between an argument and a kidnapping. I'm not prone to making up stories, you know."

"We know that," Elizabeth said soothingly.

"Call John," Martha said to Elizabeth. "Tell him to get to that hardware store. I'm sure the woman's car is still there."

"Sorry, ladies," Norman said. "No phone calls while we're in the air. Aviation law. You'll have to wait until we land."

"Don't worry," Elizabeth said. "When we get down, we'll call John. You can tell him what you saw, okay?"

"We have to find her," Martha said. "Even though I couldn't see her very well, I think she saw me looking at her. I have to wonder if she's hoping I'll help her."

Elizabeth patted Martha's hand. "We'll check it out. Don't worry."

Mary chimed in her agreement. "John will know what to do."

Martha was quiet as they headed back. She didn't want to ruin the experience for Mary by insisting she'd seen something sinister unfold on the ground below them, but she had no plans to back down. She was certain the woman had been taken against her will. She'd been kidnapped, and Martha might be the only person who could save her.

CHAPTER TWO

True to his word, Norman guided the balloon back to the festival and got them safely to the ground. During past festivals, balloon landings hadn't always fared so well. Farmers in the area were used to balloons landing in their fields due to the wind currents not cooperating with pilots. But all in all, everyone took it in good humor. The festival was a great event for the area.

The sisters waited near the entrance to the grounds, watching for John.

"It was so dark, I can't even describe the cars, let alone the victim or the kidnapper," Martha said. "I could barely make out anything at all."

"Then how could you see what happened?" Mary asked.

"The headlights from the cars."

Although Mary hadn't said it plainly, it was clear to Martha that her sister wasn't convinced that she had actually witnessed something nefarious.

Since the hardware store had closed its doors, the parking lot lights had been turned off. If they had been working, Martha might have been able to provide some kind of information that would convince her sisters she wasn't imagining things. It certainly would have allowed her to help John locate the woman.

"If it wasn't for our outside lights, we couldn't have made out our own home," Elizabeth said. "It's a wonder you saw anything at all."

"But not enough to tell John anything about the woman," Martha said. "Our only chance of helping her is to get her name from the registration of the car left in the parking lot. It shouldn't be too hard to discover."

"I'm sure that will be enough." Elizabeth put her arm around Martha. "John will find her. Try not to worry."

"Did you tell him to go straight to the hardware store?" Martha asked.

Elizabeth shook her head. "No. I have no idea if he's going there first or coming here to get more information before he heads over to Greer's."

Martha hoped he would check out the parking lot first, although she guessed it might not make much difference. As long as they found the car, John would be able to at least discover the woman's identity. Martha checked her watch again. Maybe he would call from the parking lot.

Obviously noticing her impatience, Elizabeth said, "I'm sure we'll hear from him soon."

"I would think he'd want to ask us some pertinent questions right away," Martha huffed.

"You're jumping the gun. You really have no idea what's going on. Let's have a little faith."

Martha stared at Elizabeth, who looked a little uncomfortable. "Does he doubt my story too?"

"We believe you're convinced you saw a kidnapping," Mary said. "We know you'd never make up a story like that."

"And don't worry about John," Elizabeth said. "He respects you, and I'm sure he believes you. Just be patient. He should be here any minute. Give him a chance to tell you what he's doing before you start worrying about the way he's handling things."

Elizabeth had no sooner finished speaking when John's patrol car pulled into the parking lot. He spotted the women and drove up to where they waited, then he parked, got out, and hurried toward them.

"So, go over this again," he said, looking at Martha as he approached them. "You think you witnessed a kidnapping?"

"I don't *think* I did. I know I did." Martha couldn't keep the irritation out of her voice. "You should have gone by the hardware store first. Not waited to talk to us."

John raised an eyebrow. "I did," he said. "I just came from there."

A ray of hope sprang up inside her. "Did you find the woman's car? Who is she?"

"I'm sorry, Martha, but there were no cars in the lot."

Martha stared at him. "What are you talking about? Her car has to be there." She pointed with her thumb over her shoulder. "It's the abandoned hardware store just outside of town. Greer's. Right off the highway."

"I know where it is. I'm telling you, I checked it out. There were no cars. Nothing."

"Someone must have come back for it," Martha said. She gestured toward John's car. "Take me there."

John stared at Martha for a moment without saying anything. Finally, he nodded. "All right. But without any lights in the parking lot it'll be hard to see anything."

"I don't care," Martha insisted. "I want to look for myself."

"Maybe tomorrow would be better," Elizabeth said. "When the sun's up."

"Fine," Martha said, her voice sharp. "John can take you and Mary home. I'll take the car and drive there myself."

Elizabeth sighed. "No. If you really feel this strongly about it, we'll all go."

Mary took Martha's arm. "All for one and one for all. Let's do this."

"All right," John said again. "Let's see if we can find anything that will help. If not, I'll come back in the morning and double-check the area." He looked closely at Martha. "Is there anything at all that you can tell me about the cars? About the people you saw?"

Martha shook her head. "The sun had just set. I couldn't see any details. All I saw was the woman being struck and then pushed into one of the cars."

"Could you see anything inside the vehicles?"

She sighed. "No, the angle was wrong from up there."

"Do you want to drive us all over there?" Elizabeth asked John.

"I think it would be better if we took both cars," he said. "Headlights from two cars will give us more light."

"Good thinking," Martha said. She looked at Mary. "Let's take your car. Elizabeth can go with John."

No one questioned Martha's suggestion, and soon they were all on their way to the hardware store.

"We do believe you, you know," Mary told Martha as they followed John's car.

"I'm not sure John does."

"Well, it was very difficult to see anything clearly," Mary said slowly. "I guess I can understand why he's not completely convinced."

"I suppose," Martha said with a sigh. "I'm sorry. I don't mean to be difficult. I'm just really worried about that poor woman. If her car is gone, how will we find her?"

"I don't know," Mary responded, "but we've been in tough spots before and found a way to uncover the truth."

For the first time since seeing the altercation in the parking lot, Martha was able to smile. "You're right. I've got to believe I saw her for a reason. God cares even more about this woman than we do."

Mary patted Martha's arm. "We have to trust that God will use us to rescue the woman you saw. I'm so glad we were in the right place at the right time."

"Me too."

A few minutes later, they turned in to the lot in front of the hardware store. John parked his patrol car and got out. He came up to Mary's car, and she rolled down her window.

"Can you tell me where the cars were parked?" he asked Martha.

Martha hesitated a moment, trying to remember exactly what she'd seen. She pointed toward the front of the lot. "Not far from that entrance. I'd say about forty or fifty feet back."

"Okay, why don't you park over there, a few yards from the road? Turn your lights on bright and aim them at that spot. I'll park near the entrance and do the same thing. That should give us the best illumination."

"All right," Mary said.

Martha directed Mary where to park. It didn't take long for both cars to shine their brights in a way that lit up the lot, especially the area that Martha had indicated. Once John was happy with the results, everyone exited the cars.

John pulled two flashlights from his trunk. He handed one to Martha, and Elizabeth and Mary turned on their phones' flashlights. "Try checking out the area where you saw the cars. It's not very likely anyone dropped something that will help us, but it's happened before. Maybe we'll get lucky."

John and Elizabeth went off in one direction, while Martha and Mary headed the other, all of them staying close to the area Martha had pointed out.

Martha prayed as they searched, the beams from the flashlights bouncing around. Both teams found things in the parking lot, but nothing helpful. Old candy wrappers, pop cans, fliers, and other bits of trash were soon discarded. Martha was almost ready to give up when her flashlight picked up something that sparkled. She walked toward it, bent down, and picked it up. When she realized what it was, she could feel her heart pounding in her chest.

"I found something," she called out.

Everyone gathered around her. "What is it?" John asked.

Martha held her hand out, showing him a round, gold object. "It's a charm from the Girl Scout camp I used to attend when I was a child," she said. "This award was for being helpful."

"Isn't that the same charm you got one year, Martha?" Elizabeth asked.

"Yes." She looked up at John. "I think this came off the woman's bracelet when she was accosted."

John didn't look convinced. "But it could have been here for weeks or even months, Martha. Isn't that camp closed down?"

"Yes, but there must be records somewhere. Only one girl received this charm every year." She examined the charm more closely. "It's still shiny, and there's not a scratch on it. I don't think it could have been here very long at all. So all we have to do is locate the winners of the award and find out who's missing."

"Well, I guess it's all we've got," John said. "I hope it helps us."

"We'll find her," Elizabeth said. "Good job, Martha."

Martha felt a flash of optimism. Maybe they really could find the woman. But fighting against the hope she felt was the fear that they might be too late.

CHAPTER THREE

Martha was reluctant to go to sleep Friday night. Knowing that the woman was out there somewhere, maybe injured from that blow to her head, unnerved her. But there wasn't much else the sisters could do right now. The roadways were dark, and she hadn't been able to decipher the color of either of the cars involved in the kidnapping. All she knew was that a woman had been abducted by a man. They couldn't call the scout camp, because it was closed. John had promised them he'd keep an ear to the ground. The only thing to do was go to bed and hope that daylight would bring clarity in more ways than one.

After a night of fitful sleep, Martha was relieved when morning finally arrived. She quickly got dressed and headed downstairs to start breakfast. As she entered the kitchen, Mary bustled in from taking care of the outside animals, the crisp smell of early fall lingering on her clothes.

"It's a beautiful day out there," Mary said. She grinned from ear to ear as she set her basket of eggs beside the sink. "It's a shame we'll be stuck inside most of the morning."

Elizabeth looked up from the dishes she was putting away. "I'll get out of your way in a minute, Mary, so you can wash the eggs."

"No rush," said Mary. "So long as we get the store opened on time."

Yes, the store still had to be opened, though Martha certainly didn't feel like it after a night of restless, broken sleep. But that didn't mean they couldn't squeeze in a few moments to track down some information about the missing woman. Maybe they could locate someone affiliated with the Girl Scout camp and ask about the charm. "We need to keep puzzling out the scenario from last night too," she said.

"Oh, by the way," Elizabeth said, "John called. He rechecked the parking lot once the sun was up but didn't find anything else that might help us." She put the last of the clean plates into the cupboard and stepped aside to let Mary use the sink. "Can you tell us again exactly what you saw?"

Mary ran water to rinse the eggs, one by one. "Yes, it was so dark. I don't know how you made anything out in detail from that balloon. I barely even recognized our house."

Even though it was dark, Martha knew exactly what she had seen. "A man hit a woman over the head, then pushed her into a car and drove off. I think she looked up at me for help. I think the charm fell off her bracelet."

"Are we sure the charm is meaningful?" Mary asked. "Like John said, it could have been dropped by anyone at any time."

Martha jutted her chin out. "Of course the charm is related. It has to be." If it wasn't, there was no trail to follow, and they'd never find the missing woman. She couldn't accept that.

In an obvious attempt to smooth things over, Elizabeth said, "Listen, Martha, I know you're concerned. We all are."

"We are?" Martha raised an eyebrow. She wasn't sure her sisters were as alarmed as she was.

"I know you're worried," Elizabeth repeated. She patted a chair at the table. "Why don't you sit down, and I'll make you some breakfast?"

Martha had to admit, it did sound good to take a seat and relax this morning. Elizabeth moved to the stove and began cracking some of the eggs Mary had washed into a bowl. She added cinnamon and vanilla and dipped thick slices of home-made bread into the mixture. After a few minutes of cooking, she plated up a few pieces and drizzled them with syrup before presenting them to Martha. Martha took a bite and felt her shoulders relax slightly.

"This is delicious, Elizabeth. Thank you."

Elizabeth turned and smiled at her. "You're welcome."

Mary slid into a seat at the table. "Once I got in bed last night, I started to doubt what you saw, Martha, but if you say it's true, I believe you. Now, how are we going to track down the owner of this missing charm?" She offered the question tentatively. Martha appreciated Mary's attempt to reassure her and resolved to be less harsh with her younger sister. Even though she and Mary didn't always see eye to eye, they were devoted to one another.

"Martha, I wasn't in Girl Scouts like you and Mary were," Elizabeth said. "Can you explain a little more to me about how the camp gave out these charms?"

Martha pushed the syrup bottle across the table toward Mary, who took it with a smile. "The charms were like awards. They were given out at the end of camp to the girl deemed 'most helpful,' 'best team player,' things like that. Kind of like yearbook superlatives. We would try to earn as many charms as we could for our bracelets each summer."

"But the camp is closed now, right?" asked Elizabeth.

Martha nodded. It was sad, but she'd read about the property being shut down and put up for sale several years ago. Apparently, whoever had run the place most recently had let several of the facilities fall into disrepair, and it had finally been shut down on code violations. It was a shame.

Mary took another bite of her french toast. "I wonder what happened to everything at the camp. Like the records that would show a camp roster."

"I'm hoping they were removed before the place was shut down," Martha said.

Elizabeth looked thoughtful. "Do you know anybody who worked there? Somebody who might be able to point us in the right direction to find old paperwork?"

"I don't know," Martha said slowly. "I was just a kid. All the junior counselors seemed to have nicknames, and I called all of the adults by their last names. Mrs. Jones, Mrs. Smith. My troop leader, Mrs. Bennifer, passed away years ago." She paused, tapping her fingers on the table as she thought. There had to be some way to find the information they needed. Some way to help the woman she'd seen from the hot-air balloon. "I do still keep in touch with a few of the girls I used to bunk with. I bet they could help point us in the right direction."

"That's a great idea," Elizabeth said.

Her enthusiasm made Martha feel hopeful that they'd be able to track down some information soon about who had owned the charm. It was possible she'd been wrong about her sisters not being invested in finding the missing woman.

"Maybe I could make some calls in the office if we're not too busy at the store this morning."

Mary stood and started to put away the extra food. "Fine by me. I like working the checkout counter. What a great way to spend the day, chatting with people and helping them find things."

Martha smiled. Mary was definitely a people person. The more people she had around to talk to, the happier she was.

Martha looked to Elizabeth, expecting her to parrot Mary's response, but instead, Elizabeth stood frozen in the middle of the kitchen floor. "Is something wrong?" Martha asked.

Mary rushed to Elizabeth's side. "Are you ill?"

All Elizabeth said though, was, "What day is it?"

"Oh my goodness." Mary wrung her hands. "She's having a stroke. She doesn't know what day it is."

Martha put her hands over Mary's. "Calm down. She's not having a stroke." She turned to Elizabeth. "It's Saturday."

"Saturday," Elizabeth repeated slowly. "Saturday? Oh no. I dropped the ball, girls. I'm afraid I won't be at the store this morning."

Mary tilted her head to the side. "Why not?"

"I promised Rachel I'd help her out at her variety stand on Wednesday and Saturday mornings. Only for September. I completely forgot about it until now."

"Aren't her kids helping her run the stand?"

Elizabeth grabbed her purse and jacket. "Luke, Ephraim, and the twins are helping Silas with harvest. The girls have to stay home while they prepare items for the stand and keep up with the housework. They also have to keep an eye on Anke.

She hasn't been doing well." Anke was Silas's mother and Rachel's mother-in-law, who lived with the Fischers.

"Don't worry about us at the shop," Martha said to Elizabeth. "Just tell Rachel hi for us." There was really nothing Elizabeth or Mary could do to help Martha make phone calls, and Mary was content to watch the checkout counter.

"Thanks, Martha." Elizabeth fished her car keys from her purse. "I promise I'll take some extra shifts through the week if you need me to. I'll be back at lunchtime."

Mary and Martha continued cleaning up from breakfast as Elizabeth hurried outside to her car.

The morning and early afternoon passed by quickly at the store. Martha looked up numbers for several of the women who had been involved in scouts when she was a girl. One of the women wasn't sure who had the camp records, and Martha only got voice mail for all the other ladies she knew. She left messages requesting the women get back to her. She listened for the phone all morning, anticipating a call back, but none came. Her mind remained fixated on what had happened the night before. She kept seeing the woman look up at her with what Martha imagined was a frightened, pleading glance. She just couldn't shake it.

Elizabeth returned from helping Rachel around noon. The store was steadily busy until late afternoon, when Delilah Mays walked in. Martha had left a voice mail for her. She'd been a Girl Scout leader in Bird-in-Hand for many years, but they hadn't seen her for a long time. She made her way to the counter and hugged each of the sisters in greeting.

"Martha," she said, "I'm so glad you called this morning. It is so good to see you girls again. Look at you, all grown up."

Despite her preoccupation with the missing woman, Martha felt like laughing. She wasn't sure if she'd call women in their fifties "all grown up." It seemed like a term reserved for gangly teens who had become twentysomethings, but she kept those thoughts to herself. "I wanted to talk to you about camp records—whether you might know if they were kept, and who might have them."

Delilah held up her hand. "I just ran in to pick up a gift for my sister, and then you can come to the car with me. I brought someone you'll want to talk to."

After Delilah purchased one of Luke Fischer's beautiful hand-carved breadboards, Martha followed her to the parking lot. Sitting in the passenger seat of Delilah's car was a woman with gray hair swirled into an elegant bun low on her neck. She looked to be about the same age as Delilah. As Martha and Delilah approached the car, the woman opened the door and got out to meet them.

Delilah intercepted Martha's glance. "This is the reason I came by," she said. "Do you remember Lynn? She's one of my mahjong buddies. Our group meets every Saturday for lunch, and then we go to one another's houses to play." She turned to Lynn. "Do you remember Martha?"

"Yes, Martha and I go way back. It's nice to see you again." Lynn smiled at Martha and extended her hand to shake.

Martha accepted it but felt clueless. The woman acted as if she knew her. Who was she?

"Of course," said Lynn, "you might remember me as Mrs. Smith. I think that's what you called me when I worked in the office at Camp Hollyoaks."

CHAPTER FOUR

Martha could barely believe her ears. How wonderful that Lynn Smith would come to the shop today. Maybe Martha wouldn't need information from the women she'd called earlier, after all. She had spent all morning stressing out, probably for nothing.

"Mrs. Smith, may I ask you some questions about the camp?"

The elderly woman waved her hand at Martha. "Call me Lynn, please. I'd be happy to help, but the camp is closed, you know."

"Yes, I know." Martha tried to form her question in a way that wouldn't alarm Lynn. No sense in worrying her. "I want to track down someone who used to attend the camp. Do you have any idea if records were kept after it was closed?"

"Maybe. Do you remember Mrs. Scott? Bertha Scott?"

Martha searched her memory. "I'm not sure," she said slowly.

"She was the camp secretary for many years."

Martha had a vague recollection of a woman sitting behind a desk in the office at the camp. "Oh, yes," she said. "I remember her now."

"She treated the camp records like they belonged to her personally," Lynn said. "When the camp shut down, she took them home for safekeeping, with the camp leaders' permission, of course." She frowned. "That was quite a few years ago. I can't guarantee she still has them. Even though we get together from time to time, we never talk about those old records."

"Can you tell me how to contact her?"

"She's in the phone book. Under Ralph Scott. Ralph passed away three years ago, but she hasn't changed her listing."

"Thank you so much," Martha said. "I really appreciate it."

"Bertha wouldn't have updated information about camp attendees, you know. All her information dates back to when the camp was open. I'm not sure those records will help you. The person you're looking for could have moved away years ago."

Martha hesitated a moment before telling Lynn more. "Actually, I'm not sure I know who I'm looking for. I found one of the charms we were awarded at camp in a parking lot. I'd like to find the person it belongs to."

"Well, if Bertha still has the records, that information should definitely be in there somewhere," Lynn said. "But like I said, it doesn't mean you'll be able to find the girl the charm belongs to."

Martha smiled at her. "I realize that, but I want to try. I still have a charm bracelet with my camp charms on it. They remind me of all the fun we had."

"As I remember, you only went a couple of summers, isn't that right?"

"Yes. As I got older, I decided that spending my summers doing fun things with my friends was more important. I regret that decision now. I had a great time at camp."

"Well, I hope you find the person who lost that charm," Lynn said with a smile. "It's been so nice to see you again."

"You too."

As Delilah and Lynn drove away, Martha could hardly contain her excitement. She hurried back inside the shop where Mary was helping a customer pick out an Amish quilt as a gift for her daughter's birthday, and Elizabeth was checking out a customer who was happy to have found a nice picture frame for a special family portrait. Martha waited until Elizabeth was finished before scooting up next to her and telling her about her conversation with Lynn.

"That's amazing," Elizabeth said. "So now we need to contact this Bertha Scott?"

"Yes." Martha looked at her watch. It was almost five o'clock. "Do you mind closing up while I call Bertha? I want to find out if she kept those records."

"Let us know what you find out," Elizabeth said.

Martha hurried into the house. Sure enough, she found Bertha's number in the phone book. After talking with the woman for a few minutes, she hung up and went back out to the shop. Elizabeth and Mary were straightening shelves and gathering receipts and money so they could close the shop for the day.

"I spoke to Bertha," Martha said breathlessly as she approached her sisters. "She not only has the camp records, she has lists of everyone who won charms in separate files. She's offered to loan them to me so I can go through them."

"How soon can we get them?" Elizabeth asked.

"She told me I could come by now."

"Why don't you go and fetch the files," Mary suggested, "while we finish closing up?"

"Bertha lives close to the Two Bird Café," Martha said. "I'll meet you there after I get the lists. We can have supper, look through the lists, and decide on our next move."

"Sounds like a good idea," Elizabeth said. "And I'll call John. We need to find out if the police have been notified about a missing person."

"Great," Martha said. "Call me if that's happened." She sighed. "It certainly would make things easier. Camp Hollyoaks was in business for almost fifty years. Thankfully, the charms were only awarded for around twenty of those years. Bertha said they switched to ribbons about ten years after I stopped going to camp. The charms got to be too expensive, I guess."

"That's still a lot of names to go through," Mary said with a sigh.

"I know, but unless John has something, this is all we have to go on."

"You head over to Bertha's," Elizabeth said. "We'll meet you at the Two Bird Café as soon as we can."

Martha rushed outside and got into her car. It didn't take long to find the right house. Bertha had told her it was the only pink house on the block. With white, gleaming trim, it was a darling home. Even though it had been many years since Martha had seen Bertha, she was someone easy to remember, now that Martha's memories of camp had been stirred up. A stickler for the rules, Bertha always made certain every girl checking into the camp was up on all her inoculations and had a medical release form from her parents in the files. Addresses and phone numbers were also confirmed just in case something had changed from the time the girl was initially enrolled.

Martha could still remember standing in front of Bertha's desk as she ticked through her list of requirements before Martha was allowed to check into her tent.

The so-called *tents* were huge and could hold up to six girls. The floors were cement, and steps led up into each tent. This kept them from flooding. As Martha parked her car, memories of camp filled her mind. Gathering around a large campfire singing songs, each tent group creating plays, horseback riding, hiking. She was starting to realize how much she missed those days.

Martha walked up the steps to Bertha's front door and rang the bell. She expected Bertha to answer, but instead a younger woman pulled the door open.

"Are you Martha?" she asked.

"I am."

"Mother is inside," the woman said. "I'm Debbie, her oldest daughter. Please come in."

Martha stepped inside an immaculate home. The living room was comfortable and tidy. Although Bertha was much older now, Martha would have recognized her anywhere. She still wore her hair short and combed back from her face. Her clothes were tailored and pressed, just as Martha remembered.

She held out her hand. "It's so nice to see you again, Martha," she said.

Martha shook Bertha's thin hand. "Thank you for helping me."

"Anything for our girls."

"Can I get you something to drink?" Debbie asked. "Iced tea? Coffee?"

Martha shook her head. "I'm fine, thank you."

Bertha shook her finger at Martha. "You girls. Always in a hurry." She reached over and picked up a file folder from the end table next to her. "The charms were only given during certain years," she said. "Here are the names of everyone who was awarded one. I'm sorry, they're not divided up by categories. We had awards for different things. Attendance, physical activities, earning certain badges. The charm you found. What was it for?"

"Most Helpful. I won it two years in a row."

"Yes, I remember you being very helpful," Bertha said with a smile. "Of course, some of your tentmates may have called it something else."

Martha laughed. "Like being bossy?"

"I wasn't going to say that."

"I haven't changed much. I can still be a little overbearing."

Bertha chuckled. "Mrs. Bennifer nominated you. She recognized that your desire was to help the other girls. Not just tell them what to do."

"I wish everyone was as understanding as Mrs. Bennifer," Martha said, chuckling. "She was a wonderful lady."

"Yes, she was." Bertha held out the file. "I hope you find what you're looking for."

"Thank you. I'll return this when I'm done."

Debbie, who had been listening, laughed. "You can keep it. Those are copies. Mother wouldn't let the original records out of the house even if her life was threatened. I keep trying to tell her that holding on to that information after all these years isn't necessary."

"I guess I've proven you wrong, haven't I, dear?" Bertha asked gently. "If I hadn't kept those files, the charm Martha found might not ever be returned to its owner."

After thanking Bertha and Debbie, Martha left, the file clasped in her hand. Maybe somewhere inside was the name of the woman she'd seen last night. At least now they were one step closer to finding her.

CHAPTER FIVE

"Take a seat wherever you'd like." A ponytailed waitress sped past Martha on her way to the kitchen. The aroma of cooked burgers lingered in the air, though the grill behind the counter was silent and the chef nowhere to be seen.

Martha glanced around the room. It was prime time for the dinner crowd, and the Two Bird Café wasn't especially busy. Only a quarter of the seats were taken, and most of those by single customers nursing coffees at the counter. She guessed that was a good thing. It would give her and her sisters a chance to discuss the missing woman without raising any eyebrows. Mary and Elizabeth hadn't arrived yet, so Martha slipped into a corner booth. Instead of looking at the menu, however, she pulled out the folder Bertha had given her.

The woman had kept meticulous records. Martha was impressed with how quickly Bertha had been able to locate the file with precisely the information she needed. She'd thought she was organized and efficient, but Bertha took the cake. Martha flipped open the folder and scanned the list of names inside to see if she recognized any of them.

PATTY REYNOLDS, MOST HELPFUL, 1974.

1974. The year before Martha won the same award. Patty had been one of her friends in a neighboring tent. Though she and Patty hadn't kept in close contact, Patty's daughter, Jill, had stopped by Secondhand Blessings earlier in the afternoon. If anything had happened to her mother since Friday evening, Jill would have known it. According to Jill, the two talked on the phone every morning and lived near one another.

Martha drew a line through Patty's name. Then she turned to the next name on the list, which was her own, listed twice, for 1975 and 1976. She crossed those off too, chuckling a bit to herself as she did so. But she sobered as soon as she saw the next name.

DANIELLE COLEMAN, MOST HELPFUL, 1977.

Danielle had moved away from Bird-in-Hand shortly after high school graduation to pursue a career in accounting. Martha knew she still had family in the area and came back occasionally to visit them. Was it possible Danielle was the woman who was abducted? Maybe she'd been visiting family for the weekend and had gotten mixed up in something she shouldn't have. The thought gave Martha chills. Could it have been Danielle's upturned, pleading face she'd spied from the hot-air balloon?

Martha circled Danielle's name. She'd just started to move down the list when Mary and Elizabeth appeared, sliding into the empty side of the booth.

"Did you learn anything from Bertha?" asked Mary, just as the ponytailed waitress walked up to their table to take their drink orders. They all ordered iced tea, though Martha took hers without sugar, the same way she liked her coffee.

As the waitress walked away, Martha slid the list toward her sisters. "Bertha gave me a list of the names of the women who earned the charm we found before the camp switched to giving out ribbons for awards."

Elizabeth pressed her lips together but accepted the list.

"What?" Martha asked. Elizabeth didn't have the look of someone on a mission. Instead, she appeared doubtful. "You said you believed what I told you."

Elizabeth sighed. "I do believe you. I just—"

"What?" Martha asked again, a little more impatiently this time.

Elizabeth's voice was gentle. "I just hope we're not on a wild goose chase. We don't even know for sure that the charm is linked to that woman's disappearance. This could be a huge waste of time."

Martha huffed out a breath. What else did they have to go on? They had to find the woman. Who knew the amount of danger she was in? "Maybe it is a shot in the dark, but I feel like it's the only clue we have until we hear more from John. Did you find out if a missing person report has been filed?"

Elizabeth shook her head. "I'm sorry, Martha. Of course you're right. And no, John said nothing's been reported at the station yet. He'll let us know right away if he hears anything though."

Elizabeth's apology mollified Martha, but she still felt on edge. When her drink arrived, she took a long, cooling sip of iced tea.

Mary squinted at the list before pointing at a name farther down. "You can check off Vanessa Lagesse. I just saw her raking leaves in her yard as we passed by on our way to meet you. And Lena Gibson. She was filling up at the gas station."

"No," Elizabeth corrected. "You're thinking of someone else. That was Eleanor Parker. They have that similar hairstyle now."

Mary tilted her head to one side. "I don't know. Are you sure?" She slid the list back across the table to Martha. "Hmm, I guess you're right. Keep Lena on the list."

Martha sighed. "That only leaves about...oh...sixteen people to account for."

"It'll be okay," Elizabeth said. "We'll whittle the list down." She pointed to the name directly below Danielle's. "What about Darlene O'Neal? Doesn't she work here at the café?"

Their waitress reappeared with their drinks. But before she could take their food orders, Elizabeth asked her if Darlene was still employed at the café.

"I don't know," said the waitress. "I just started filling in on the weekends. I can go check though, if you want."

"Thank you. That would be great," Mary said.

The waitress smiled. "Not a problem. I'll be right back. Can I get your food orders before I go?"

"Sure. I'll have the Sunrise Special." Mary smothered a laugh. "I guess it's kind of late in the day to order that, isn't it?"

The waitress smiled again. "I'm a fan of breakfast for dinner too." She jotted the order down and turned to Elizabeth and Martha. "And for you ladies?"

Elizabeth ordered the chicken sandwich with a side salad, and Martha chose a bunless hamburger and sweet potato wedges.

"How do you do that?" Mary asked Martha in wonderment.

"Do what?"

"Eat a burger without the bun. It just seems—wrong."

Martha shrugged. "I don't know. Just trying to watch my carbs. The older I get the faster what I eat shows up on my hips." It wasn't easy counting carbs with all the baked goods she made each week for the store. Almond flour just didn't provide quite the same texture as regular flour. She'd stayed strong though, until she'd made a beautiful lemon chiffon cake. She was a sucker for citrus. All her dieting resolve had melted with one whiff of the tangy frosting. Nowadays, she watched what she ate when it was convenient.

Mary shuddered. "I'll stick with my carbs, thanks very much."

"To each his own," said Elizabeth. "Or her own, in this case."

Martha made a good-natured grimace at Mary as another, older waitress approached their table. Her nametag read MYRTLE. "You ladies were asking about Darlene?"

"Yes, does she still work here?" Martha asked.

"Sure does. She's not working tonight though. She called in a few minutes ago. Said she needed time off to take care of her sister who has some kind of wicked stomach bug. Sounds like what my little grandson has. He's been out of school for a week, and it just started, poor kid."

"I've heard there's something going around," Elizabeth said.

The waitress frowned at her. "Don't you ladies run that secondhand shop not far from here?"

"Yes," Martha said. "Have you been in our store?"

The waitress smiled. "Yeah. I bought a microwave there. Been workin' great."

"Happy to hear that," Elizabeth said with a smile.

The waitress nodded and walked back behind the counter.

"Hmm," said Mary. "Sounds like Darlene is accounted for. Who else is on the list, Martha?"

Martha read off a few more names. Together, the sisters weeded out the names of people they'd seen since Friday night. Some had come into the store, and others had been out and about in town. They slowly narrowed down the list.

"What do we do next?" asked Mary. "Go knock on doors?"

"Maybe make some phone calls?" Elizabeth suggested. "We could just tell people about the charm we found. Mention that we're trying to find the owner so we can return it."

"That's a good idea," Martha said.

Elizabeth's phone buzzed, and she fished it out of her purse. "It's John." She answered the call, and after a brief conversation, hung up. Her eyes were wide. "We may have a lead."

"Did John find something?" asked Martha. Her throat felt tight, and the sensation only heightened with Elizabeth's next words.

"I'd say he did," Elizabeth said. "A missing person report has been filed."

CHAPTER SIX

W ho was it?" Martha's heart pounded. "Who was the report filed for?"

Elizabeth dropped her phone back into her bag. "For a teen girl named Olivia Acosta. Does that ring any bells for you?"

Mary shook her head. Martha scanned Bertha's list, even though she knew she wouldn't find Olivia's name on it. The teen was likely too young to have attended the camp at all before it closed, and she definitely wouldn't have been the original owner of the charm. So what did that mean? Either the charm had been lost before Friday night and wasn't a clue at all—or things were connected in a different way than Martha realized. The waitress brought their food to the table, and after saying grace, Martha dug in with gusto. She was really hungry.

"Your missing woman couldn't be a teenager, could she?" Elizabeth asked Martha.

"Yes, she could have been," Martha said. "I couldn't see her clearly."

"So the charm has nothing to do with the abduction," Mary said. "Olivia couldn't have attended the camp. She's too young."

"But what if it was passed down," Martha said. "You know, from a grandmother or mother? Olivia could still be the person we're looking for."

Elizabeth frowned. "Or anyone could have bought it at a pawn shop. Or picked it up at a yard sale. And if that's how the missing woman got the charm, then this list is useless."

"But why would anyone buy a charm like that, Elizabeth?" Mary asked. "It wouldn't mean anything to anyone else. I think it either belongs to someone on this list or to someone she's related to. Maybe this Olivia really is the person Martha saw."

Martha sighed. "I hope you're right. If we could connect the charm with a missing person, John could get involved. Things would move a lot faster."

Mary and Elizabeth had just started to eat their food when Elizabeth's phone rang once more. "Hello?" She spoke for a few minutes and then ended the call. "Well, our progress was short-lived, I'm afraid."

"Was that about the missing teenager?" Mary asked.

"Yes, except she's not missing anymore. Apparently, Olivia got mad at her mom and left without telling anyone. She stayed with a friend Friday night, and no one knew about it. She's back home now."

Martha let out a breath. So the woman they were looking for was still out there somewhere. Back to square one. She cast another glance at the list in front of her. "We need to start making some phone calls. Do either of you know any of the other women on this list? I think I still have contact info for Danielle Coleman, but we'll have to go home first. Her information is in my address book."

Mary frowned and turned to Elizabeth. "Apparently, I don't know Lena Gibson as well as I thought I did. Are you sure that wasn't her?"

"One hundred percent sure. Didn't you notice the passel of dogs yipping from the back seat? Lena is allergic to dogs. Remember that time she visited us and started sneezing uncontrollably, even though the animals were all outside? I saw her the next day, and one of her eyes was swollen shut. Unless Lena is taking some miracle allergy shots, the lady at the gas station was definitely Eleanor Parker."

Mary sighed. "I forgot about her allergy. I guess you're right."

"Do you know anything about Lena?" asked Martha. "Does she still live around here?"

"I think she does," Elizabeth said. "She used to live just down from the post office. In that cute little three-story home with the attic dormer?"

"Perfect," Martha said, setting her fork down with a clatter. "We can stop by there on the way home."

"Stop by?" Mary looked at her, dumbfounded. "What are we gonna do? Go up to the door and ask if she's been kidnapped lately?"

Martha rolled her eyes. "No, we won't do that. I'm pretty sure she lives alone. We're just looking to see if there are lights on at her house, or any activity." She swung her purse strap up over one shoulder. "Are you all done eating yet?"

"One more bite," Mary said, scooping up a forkful of hash browns covered with cheese. "This is delicious."

"Can you get a to-go box? This is important." Martha couldn't understand why her sisters weren't taking the kidnapping as seriously as she was. They had to find the woman, and soon. The quicker they whittled down the list, the better.

Mary and Elizabeth exchanged glances. "I guess I can," Mary said. She flagged down the waitress for a box while Elizabeth paid for the meal at the register.

As they exited the restaurant Elizabeth offered to ride with Martha and let Mary take her car. Martha turned the key in the ignition, and immediately, an orange light in the shape of an old-fashioned oil can popped up on the dashboard. "You need an oil change?" asked Elizabeth. "I'm surprised. You're usually so punctual with things like that."

Martha waved off her sister's comment. She'd had a lot going on and hadn't had time to drop off her car for maintenance. "I'll take it in soon."

"All right," said Elizabeth. "Just make sure you do. It can be a real issue if you put it off."

Martha fought off a flicker of annoyance. Even though Elizabeth was older than she was, Martha had always been the most responsible of the sisters. If anything needed to be done, she did it. She didn't need a reminder from Elizabeth, even if she was well meaning.

Martha followed Mary's lead as she pulled off into the post office's empty parking lot. Then Mary got out of her vehicle and climbed into Martha's car so they could all watch Lena's house together. "Which one is hers?" asked Martha.

Elizabeth pointed down the street at a pretty red-bricked house with tall windows and black shutters. The lights were all off, except one light in a downstairs window. "That's Lena's house. Her husband passed away a few years ago. No pets, obviously, unless she has reptiles or something like that." She shuddered. "Who would ever keep a snake or a lizard for a pet anyway? I wouldn't exactly think they'd make cozy companions."

Mary motioned to Martha. "Can you turn off your lights? We look so conspicuous. What are we going to say if Lena comes out in her yard in a robe and slippers and sees us, sitting down the street gawking at her?"

Martha turned off her headlights. After a few minutes the sisters watched as an elderly woman stepped cautiously out onto the front porch. Her wiry hair stuck up in tufts, as if she'd been sleeping on it, but she wore a nice outfit—a blouse and slacks with loafers. The woman looked around for a few minutes as though gathering her bearings, then she shuffled down the steps and turned onto the sidewalk that threaded in front of the house.

"Who is that?" asked Elizabeth. "It's not Lena."

"Where's she going? And where's Lena?" asked Martha. The second question was answered almost immediately, as Lena burst out the front door and raced down the steps. "Mom! Stop! Stay on the sidewalk! You'll get hit!" She yelled after the elderly woman, who had made her way farther from the house. The woman turned for a split second, looking confused. Then she continued walking.

"Mom! It's me, Lena! Stop!"

"Something's wrong. We need to help," said Elizabeth, unbuckling her seat belt and opening her door. Martha started to slide out too, but suddenly froze, watching in horror.

The elderly woman pivoted off the sidewalk and stepped directly into the busy street.

CHAPTER SEVEN

Elizabeth sprinted from the car toward the woman, pulling her out of the street just seconds before a car roared past them. The driver was a teenager who obviously hadn't expected anyone to step out in front of his car. His wide eyes and frightened expression probably matched Elizabeth's. The young man braked, got out of the car, and looked back at them. After seeing that everyone was safe, he took off down the street, much slower this time.

"Mom, are you all right?" Lena came running toward them, fear distorting her features.

"She's fine, Lena," Elizabeth said. She had to take a few deep breaths to calm herself. If she hadn't pulled Lena's mother out of the way, would she have been hit? Although she couldn't be certain, it was a distinct possibility.

"Elizabeth?" Lena asked as she put her arm around her confused mother. "Is that you?"

"Yes, it's me," Elizabeth said as Martha and Mary ran up next to them.

"Martha? Mary?" Lena said, her voice shaking. "I have no idea why you're here, but thank God you were." She met Elizabeth's eyes. "Thank you so much. If you hadn't pulled Mom from the street…" Although she didn't finish her sentence, it was clear what she was thinking. What they were all probably thinking.

"Can we help you get your mom back inside?" Elizabeth asked. She didn't feel the need to explain to Lena why they were outside her house. It was a long story, and it was clear Lena needed to take care of her mother.

"Would you like to come in for a while?" Lena asked. Her mother tried to wriggle from her daughter's grasp. "It's okay, Mom," Lena said gently. "We're going back inside."

"I need to go home," the old woman insisted.

"You are home," Lena said, patiently. "You live here now."

"No, this isn't my house."

"Why don't we talk later?" Elizabeth suggested. "You need to tend to your mother."

"Are you sure we can't help you?" Martha asked, repeating Elizabeth's previous offer.

Lena shook her head. "We're fine." She sighed. "I was sure the front door was locked. Mom has Alzheimer's. I'm trying to take care of her, but it's difficult." Her eyes washed over with tears.

Elizabeth put her hand on Lena's arm. "If there's anything we can do, all you have to do is ask."

Lena's voice shook as she said, "Thank you, but what you did tonight… I can never thank you enough…." Her voice faded.

"I'll call you next week," Elizabeth said. "We can catch up."

"I'd like that," Lena said. "I'd better get Mom in the house. God bless you."

The sisters stood on the sidewalk and watched until Lena and her mother were safe inside and the door closed behind them.

"Well, Lena isn't our missing person," Martha said, "but I'm certainly glad we drove by her house when we did."

"Me too," Mary said. "I think God sent us here."

"I do too," Elizabeth said. She blew out a deep breath. "Let's head home. This was enough excitement for one night."

"I agree," Mary said.

Martha sighed. "I guess you're right." Elizabeth could tell she was disappointed.

Mary caught Elizabeth's arm, and they stopped walking as Martha continued to the cars. "I wish she didn't take this so personally," she said.

"She's just afraid we don't believe her," Elizabeth said. "So even if we're not sure what actually happened, we need to give her our support. Martha is really worried." She gave Mary a quick hug. "We need to trust her, Mary. Martha is very level-headed, and I believe her."

Mary sighed. "It's not that I doubt her story, but how can we know for certain we're on the right track with this charm? Anyone could have left it there."

"Maybe we can find the owner. And that will be a blessing even if she's not missing, right?"

Mary smiled. "I guess so. It's not that late. Let's work on the list when we get home."

Elizabeth headed back to the car, glad to have her sisters on the same page for once.

The sisters were quiet on the drive back from church the next morning. Pastor Nagle's sermon was about serving others with actual deeds—not just lip service. Elizabeth felt even more convicted about finding the woman Martha thought had been abducted.

When they got inside the house, Martha began making sandwiches for lunch. Elizabeth retrieved the list of people who had been awarded charms and started going through it. Several names had been knocked off last night by a few phone calls. Martha was able to reach Danielle Coleman, whose married name was Danielle Mills, so her name was crossed off. This morning, two of the women on the list were at church. The sisters were now down to six names.

Mary put a pitcher of iced tea on the table, along with glasses full of ice. Then she sat down. "Who's left?" she asked Elizabeth.

"Evelyn Mercer, Cindy Lister, Kathryn McConnell, Betty Steele, Paula Minton, and Deidre Ruble." Elizabeth sighed. "I know that Evelyn's last name is Davis now, and Betty's married name is Bridges. But I'm not sure of the others." She frowned. "Didn't Paula move away when she was young?"

"I believe she did," Martha said as she carried a plate of sandwiches to the table. "Her sister still lives here. We could check with her." She put the plate on the table. "Did anyone bring in the paper?"

"I did this morning when I fed the animals. It's over there." Mary gestured toward the counter.

Martha, who liked reading the paper on Sundays after church, walked over and picked it up before sitting down with her sisters. She looked at Elizabeth. "You can mark Cindy Lister off the list. I talked to her cousin at church. She's fine. She and her husband moved to Philadelphia to take care of his mother."

Elizabeth drew a line through Cindy's name. After saying grace, the sisters began eating.

"So how many names are left?" Martha asked.

"Five," Elizabeth said.

"Are we asking everyone if they've lost their charm from camp?" Martha asked.

"I have been," Elizabeth said. "Everyone had theirs except for a couple of people who had no idea what happened to it. But they misplaced it years ago."

"I'm afraid I haven't checked on the charm with everyone I spoke to," Mary said. "I've been focusing on finding someone who's missing."

"Don't you think that's important?" Martha asked with a frown. "I mean, if the charm has nothing to do with what I saw, we need to find that out."

"I agree," Elizabeth said. "And like we said, we still might be able to return the charm to its owner."

"I still believe the woman who was kidnapped left it behind," Martha said emphatically. "The hardware store probably swept their lot regularly when they were open. They've only been closed a few months. Sure, maybe it was lost shortly after it closed, but I doubt it. It was lying in plain sight. It wasn't covered up by trash or swept into the street by all that rain we had last month. And it didn't look like it'd been lying on the ground for a long time."

Elizabeth considered Martha's argument. "Makes sense, Martha. Let's see if we can knock these last names off our list after lunch." She smiled at her sister. "We'll keep going until we find our missing woman."

Martha returned her sister's smile and flipped open the newspaper. As she perused the front page, her eyes widened. A few seconds later, she gasped.

"Martha, is everything all right?" Mary asked.

Martha turned the newspaper around so her sisters could see it. On the front page were several pictures of balloons from the night before. Their balloon was in the middle of the page.

"That's really neat," Elizabeth said, "but why did you react like that?"

Martha pointed at the text below the pictures. "It says these pictures were taken by a drone." She stabbed her finger at the photo of their balloon. "Look where this was taken. It's almost directly over the hardware store. What if the drone captured footage of the kidnapping? Maybe this will help us figure out who was abducted and how we can find her!"

CHAPTER EIGHT

"Can I see the paper, please?" asked Mary, and Martha handed it over. Mary looked at the front-page article about the balloon festival. Then she flipped a few pages into the edition and held the paper up as Martha had. "Look at this. There's another article about the drone operator. It turns out it was a local teen who's into tech stuff."

Mary read the article out loud. "'Cody Stephens is a freshman at Conestoga Valley High School, but despite his age, he's no stranger to entrepreneurship. The fourteen-year-old has owned and operated his own video imaging company for the past year and has only recently delved into drone technology. He is currently president of the Robotics Club at his school, under the leadership of long-time science teacher, Mr. Alex Wright.'"

Mary looked up from the paper. "That name sounds familiar. Alex Wright. If that's who I think it is, we went to school together."

Martha immediately left the room to grab the phone book from a shelf in the office. Excitement rose up inside her. They had another lead to investigate. It gave her hope that they could find the woman they'd been searching for.

"Martha, where are you going?" Elizabeth's voice drifted down the hall. Martha returned to the kitchen with the white pages clutched in her hand.

"I'm looking up Alex Wright's number. Mary, you said you know him, right?"

"I said I *knew* him," Mary corrected. "A long time ago when we were kids. I haven't talked to him in years."

"Well, now's a perfect time to get reacquainted," Martha said. She handed the phone and the phone book to her sister.

"The school won't be open today," Mary said. "I'll have to wait until tomorrow morning to call."

Martha let out a frustrated breath of air. "You can call him at home, can't you?"

"I might be free-spirited, but I'm not that forward." Mary pushed the book back across the table to Martha. "I'm not going to call a single man on his day off, not even to ask him about some missing woman."

"How do you know he's single?" Elizabeth asked with a little grin.

Mary shrugged and looked embarrassed. "Oh, people talk. You know all the little old ladies at the hairdresser. Information spreads like wildfire."

Martha still hoped she could talk Mary into it. "I'm sure no one would mind you calling about something as important as a missing person, Mary."

Before Mary could answer, there was a knock at the door, and Elizabeth answered it. It was John.

Elizabeth opened the door and waved him inside. "John, what a nice surprise. Why don't you come in and have a sandwich? We were just having lunch."

"No, thanks. I already ate. I wouldn't be opposed to a strong cup of coffee though."

"Sure." Elizabeth poured him a cup of coffee and brought it to the table where he'd sat down.

He took a few sips then leaned back in his chair. "Thank you. That does me good."

"I don't guess you've heard anything about another missing person?" Martha couldn't help but ask right away.

John didn't seem taken aback by Martha's bluntness though. "No, the only report we've had was the one I told you about for Olivia Acosta."

"How did they find Olivia so quickly?" Mary asked. "The report was filed just a few minutes before you called back."

"Apparently, Olivia turned herself in almost right away," John said. "As soon as her mom filed the report, she and Olivia's friends started sharing the situation on social media. Olivia was hunkered down at her friend's house, and when she saw all the fuss, she realized things had gotten out of control. She got worried she'd be in trouble with the law, so she called her mom. The last I heard, Olivia was back home, and the family had reconciled."

"I'm glad that story ended well," Elizabeth said.

"I am too," said John. "They don't always."

Martha shuddered. She could only pray their case would turn out all right. "I just can't believe no one has heard anything about that poor woman. I saw the kidnapping happen right in front of my eyes. That woman was obviously being taken somewhere against her will."

John took another long drink from his mug and placed it on the table. "It is a serious matter, and I promise I'm keeping an ear to the ground for any information. If anything sinister occurred, word of it should turn up sooner rather than later. People can't keep secrets, you know. Especially not in a tight-knit community."

Martha adjusted her position in the chair. "That's good to know, but in the meantime, we'll just continue working through our list of names."

"Ah, yes, the list. Elizabeth told me about that. Making any progress?"

"Some."

Mary finished her last bite of sandwich. "We have it down to a handful of people."

"Anybody I would know?"

"Maybe." Martha pulled the list from her pocket and began reading the names from the top down. "Evelyn Davis. Kathryn McConnell. Paula Minton. Deidre Ruble."

She looked up at John to see if he recognized any of the names, but he just shook his head. Martha continued down the list. "Betty Steele. I understand her last name is Bridges now."

To Martha's surprise, John laughed. "Now, I do know Betty. We just had a doozy of a story come through the station about her." He took another sip of coffee and shook his head while continuing to chuckle. "We got an early morning call yesterday from her husband, Jerry, who said his truck had been stolen."

"That doesn't sound very funny," Elizabeth said.

"Oh, wait. It gets better. We asked if Jerry had any idea who could have stolen it, and he said he certainly did. His wife."

"His wife?"

"Yep. Apparently, Betty left a note for her husband saying he took her for granted and she was tired of it. Said she felt like he paid more genuine attention to, and I quote—'his piece of junk Chevy'—than to her. So she took the truck and left to stay at her sister's house in Witmer until he got his priorities straight."

"What happened after that?" Elizabeth asked.

John continued. "Well, I told the guy he couldn't report his truck as stolen when his wife's name was on the title, but he wouldn't listen to me. He was so fired up, I thought he'd have a conniption on the spot."

"Are you certain he was telling the truth?" Martha couldn't help but be a little suspicious. Unless she had a personal confirmation that each woman on the list was safe, she couldn't relax. What if Jerry had made a big fuss about his wife taking his truck because he'd been involved in her disappearance? What if he was trying to throw the police off the trail by claiming he was the victim? It was a perfect distraction, a smoke screen to explain his wife's sudden absence.

"I don't have any reason to believe he's not," John said.

Martha penciled in a question mark next to Betty's name.

John finished his coffee and took the cup to the sink. "Thank you, ladies, for the conversation and the hospitality. I have some things to take care of, so I'm afraid I'm going to have to head out."

"Have a restful Sunday," Elizabeth said as she saw him to the door. Martha watched her sister's gaze follow John as he left. She knew Elizabeth cared for him but strongly desired that he be a Christian before they committed to a relationship with each other. They'd seen some evidence in recent months that his attitude toward God had softened dramatically, and she knew Elizabeth was hopeful he'd come to have an authentic, personal relationship with Jesus. Elizabeth closed the door and returned to the table to sit down again.

"Well, it sounds like we're down one more name on our list," she said.

"I don't know. Are we?" Mary asked.

Martha was glad to see her younger sister was thinking like her.

"I feel like we should check up on Mr. Bridges's story, just to make sure his wife is really where he says she is."

Elizabeth nodded. "All right, we can look into that tomorrow. And Mary, you can call the science teacher...what was his name again?"

"Alex Wright."

"Right. Mr. Wright." Elizabeth smiled at her own joke.

Mary groaned. "Very funny. As if this situation wasn't already a little awkward."

"I'm just kidding. It was too good to pass up."

Elizabeth and Mary kept up the friendly banter, but Martha's heart wasn't so light anymore. All she could think about was waking up the next morning to continue the search for the missing woman.

CHAPTER NINE

During a slow period in the shop Monday morning, Mary called the school to see if Alex Wright was available. She could see Martha straining to listen, but she didn't mind. Although she felt odd calling someone she hadn't spoken to in three decades, she couldn't help but wonder if the drone had recorded something that might help them. It was a long shot, but Martha was so convinced she'd seen someone kidnapped, Mary had become a believer. At first, she'd questioned her sister's story. Not that Martha would lie. She wouldn't. Nor was she given to flights of fancy. But everyone could make a mistake when viewing something from so far away—in the dark. What if she simply witnessed a lover's quarrel? Maybe the woman was just fine. Of course, if the man involved actually had hit her and shoved her into a car... Well, that was just wrong. And then there was the question as to why the woman's car was missing. The whole thing certainly was suspicious. As she waited for Alex to come on the line, she thought about the times Martha had supported her. Believed in her. She looked over at Martha's concerned expression. She was really worried. Now, so was Mary.

"Hello?"

Alex's voice startled her. For a moment she forgot who she'd called. She cleared her throat. "Alex? This is Mary Classen Baxter. Do you remember me?"

Alex's rich laugh came over the phone. "Of course I do. Bird-in-Hand isn't that big, you know."

Mary chuckled. "No, it's not, but it's been a long time since we've had a chance to talk."

"True. Is there something I can help you with?"

"I saw the article in Sunday's paper about your student. The one who took the drone footage?"

"You mean Cody?" Alex asked. "He's something else. I don't think I've ever had such a promising student."

Although his praise was effusive, Mary heard hesitation in his voice. "Is something wrong?" she asked.

Alex sighed. "I can't really discuss students' personal lives with anyone, but let's just say I'd like to see more involvement from his family."

"I'm sorry to hear that."

"It happens," he replied. "Some parents think working long hours and making a lot of money is the best way to help their kids." He paused a moment before saying, "So what is it about Cody's pictures that you're interested in?"

"It's not his pictures, per se," Mary said. "My sister Martha saw someone being assaulted Friday evening at the festival. We were in one of the balloons at the time. Yesterday we saw the pictures Cody took in the paper. We noticed that some of Cody's footage was taken near the spot where Martha saw this happen. We're wondering if Cody might have inadvertently recorded something that might help us."

"Well, I guess anything is possible."

"Are the pictures in the paper the only photos he took?" Mary asked, hoping there were more.

"Yes," Alex said, "but we still have the video footage."

"I...I confess I don't know much about this," Mary said slowly. "How do you get pictures from drone video footage?"

"Look, I'd love to explain it to you, but I have to get to class. Why don't you meet me for lunch so we can talk more?"

"Can you hold on a moment? Not sure I can get away."

"Sure."

Before Mary could finish telling Martha and Elizabeth about Alex's invitation to lunch, they were both nodding.

"You held down the fort on Saturday," Elizabeth said. "Meet him for lunch, and if you need more time, just take it. Get back when you can."

Mary could hear the urgency in Elizabeth's voice. She was clearly worried about the woman Martha saw Friday night. Mary put the phone back to her ear. "It's fine. Where do you want to meet?"

"El Ranchero? About twelve fifteen?"

"Sounds good. I'll see you then." Mary ended the call and put her phone in her pocket. Although she didn't really care where they ate, she loved El Ranchero's Mexican food. Their tamales were handmade and were the best Mary had ever tasted.

"So does he think there might be something on the video footage?" Martha asked as Mary walked over to where she stood.

Mary shrugged. "He's not sure. I'll find out what I can at lunch." She started to tell Martha more about her conversation with Alex when the front doors slid open and some people came in. Probably tourists. Martha went over to talk to them while Mary checked on an elderly woman who appeared to be interested in their selection of slow cookers. The woman was confused about the different sizes and functions of slow cookers. It took several minutes to find something that would meet her needs. When the woman left, she had a smile on her face.

Mary realized with a start that she should already be on her way to the restaurant. She'd gotten so interested in helping the customer, she'd lost track of time. She grabbed her jacket, said goodbye to her sisters, and headed out the door. Even though she was afraid she'd be late, she pulled into El Ranchero's parking lot right at twelve fifteen. The lot was pretty full, but then someone who'd parked near the entrance pulled out. Mary took the spot and hurried into the restaurant. There were people waiting to be seated. She glanced around the dining room, hoping to see Alex. She heard someone call her name, and she was grateful to see that he had secured a table.

"So glad to see you," Alex said, standing as Mary scooted into her chair. When she was settled in, he sat down as well.

"You too." Mary smiled at him, suddenly feeling a little nervous. Alex was a handsome man. Mary had heard through word of mouth that quite a few single women in Bird-in-Hand had set their cap for him. She could certainly see why. At that moment, Bill Richmond's face drifted into her mind, but she mentally shook the image away.

"So what do you like here?" Alex asked.

Mary grinned. "I'm crazy about their tamales. They're made from scratch. You can't beat them."

Alex quickly perused the menu. "Here's the tamale dinner. Comes with sweet corn tomalito and rice."

"The tomalito is incredible."

Alex closed his menu. "You're right. I love that. This might be the fastest I've ever made up my mind. Thanks."

Mary laughed. "I usually take a while too, but not when I come here." She looked around the charming restaurant decorated in reds, greens, and golds. The owners had tried hard to make the atmosphere fit the food. In Mary's opinion, they'd done a great job. Wonderful aromas drifted from the kitchen, and Mary realized how hungry she actually was.

"So you have some questions about the footage Cody took the night of the balloon festival?"

"Yes." She frowned. "How does someone go about getting pictures from a video? Sorry, I'm really clueless when it comes to almost anything technical."

"There's a process, but I don't think knowing about it will help you. All we need to do is go through the footage. If you see something of interest, we can take a screenshot of it and print it. Hopefully, we'll find a clue that will point you in the right direction. Of course, the footage belongs to Cody. He'll have to agree to let you see it."

"Do you think he'll mind?"

Before Alex could respond, a waitress came up to their table to take their order. After she walked away, Alex said, "I don't know. Cody's had a tough time. I told you a little about his parents. He has a pretty big chip on his shoulder." He was quiet for a moment. "Look, why don't you come to the science fair tonight at the school? I'll introduce you. It'll give you an opportunity to get to know Cody and explain why you need his help."

"A science fair in September?" Mary asked. "The kids haven't been in school long enough for that, have they?"

"These are students who took a special class over the summer. Some of the most exceptional kids in the school." Alex shrugged. "I'm hoping Cody will be willing to help you once you meet him."

"I guess I'm confused," Mary said. "I understand this boy has some problems, but why wouldn't he want to help? I mean, if someone was kidnapped…"

Alex frowned and held up his hand, stopping Mary from continuing.

"Just a minute. I thought you said your sister saw a person being assaulted. This person was kidnapped? If that's true, why aren't the police looking for suspects?"

Mary explained that there were no missing person reports, so there wasn't much the police could do. "We think the person who was abducted left a clue. A charm from an old Girl Scout camp that's closed now. We're going through lists of women who won the charm, trying to find the person Martha saw Friday night. But if Cody recorded something that could identify her—or her abductor…"

"You'd have a much better chance of finding her quickly?"

"Exactly."

Alex was silent as the waitress brought the iced teas they'd ordered. "Well," he said when she left, "I guess we'd better convince Cody to let you go through that footage. Will you come tonight? To the science fair? It's from seven to nine in the school gym."

Mary nodded. "I'll be there."

"I can't promise anything, Mary," Alex said, "but I'll do my best to convince Cody to help you."

Mary breathed a sigh of relief. Was it possible they might find something that would lead them to the kidnapped woman? All she could do was hope Cody Stephens would lead them in the right direction. Right now, they needed all the help they could get.

CHAPTER TEN

M artha kept one eye trained on the front door of Secondhand Blessings as she tidied shelves. Mary still hadn't returned from her lunch meeting with Alex Wright, and Martha was eager to hear what she had discovered. Maybe they'd get a break in the case. She and Elizabeth had continued talking about the small list of women who had won the Most Helpful charm from Camp Hollyoaks, in between assisting customers. Elizabeth had made a couple of phone calls and found out that Paula Minton was at her sister's, and Evelyn Davis moved away years ago. They'd whittled the list down to only three names, and Martha couldn't wait for the shop to close at five so they could try to track down the remaining women.

Elizabeth returned from the back room, where she'd taken a phone call. "Was that one of the Figges?" asked Martha. The newly married couple, Kenny and Joni Figge, had a nice-sized farm on the outskirts of Bird-in-Hand and had expressed interest in selling some gently used horse tack to the store. They hadn't really carried anything like that before, but Martha imagined it would sell well if they could find a proper way to display it. She'd contacted Bill Richmond earlier in the week about building a special rack for it.

"No, it wasn't a customer," Elizabeth said. "It was John, calling from the station. He said Betty Steele isn't our missing lady.

She left her sister's house this morning and is back home now. The truck is too." She smiled. "I imagine it was a lot easier for missing people to stay…well, missing…before all this technology took over. Now, a person is just a phone call away."

"Or a social media account away." Martha couldn't help but think of Olivia Acosta. "So that leaves just two on the list."

Elizabeth walked to the front counter and smoothed out the dog-eared list. She crossed off Betty's name and then looked up. "Right. Kathryn O'Connell and Deidre Ruble."

Just then, Mary entered the store, bringing a breeze of crisp air with her through the pneumatic doors. "How would you all like to go out on the town tonight?"

Elizabeth laughed. "I don't know that I've ever been 'out on the town,' as you call it. What does that even mean? Please tell me we're not chaperoning you and Alex on a date."

Mary turned red. "I don't know where you're getting these silly ideas. Alex is very nice, but I'm not interested in him, at least not romantically. I wanted to see if you'd be interested in attending a science fair at the Conestoga Valley High School. It's later in the evening, so that should give us plenty of time to close up the shop and eat supper before we go."

"What's so important about the science fair?" Elizabeth asked.

"Alex said he'll introduce us to Cody there, and we can ask him about the drone footage."

"Alex who?"

Bill Richmond entered the store, lugging an apparatus that looked like a sawhorse. Mary's head snapped up. "Oh, nobody," she said quickly. "Hi, Bill."

"Hello, Mary." He tugged at an imaginary hat brim at her and grinned. Then he turned toward Martha. "I have a special delivery for you."

Martha gasped. "Don't tell me you already made that display stand for the horse tack?" She hadn't expected the job to be completed so quickly, but Bill was nothing if not an efficient worker.

"The long bar in the middle holds saddles," he said, pointing toward the stand. "The poles on the sides have hooks to display harnesses and reins, things like that. I kept it pretty simple, so the merchandise takes center stage, but I can change anything you need me to."

Martha shook her head. "No, it's perfect. Thank you so much. How much do we owe you?"

"On the house," said Bill, smiling at Mary as he left. She watched him go and didn't look up when Elizabeth cleared her throat.

"Now, what were you saying about the drone footage, Mary?" Elizabeth asked. Mary was staring after Bill with a wistful look on her face.

"Hello? Earth to Mary?" Martha waved her hand in front of her sister's eyes.

Mary blinked. "I'm sorry. What were we talking about?"

"The drone footage," Martha said. "Is Cody going to help us?"

Mary shook her head as if to clear her thoughts. "Oh, that. I'm not sure yet. We're meeting up with him at the science fair."

"Well, that's perfect timing," Elizabeth said. "We only have two names left. Maybe this will point us to the woman we're looking for."

Martha didn't respond to Elizabeth's comment, just continued thinking. Would the footage show a woman not on their list? Was their list worth anything at all? Were they on the right track, or had they been sidelined by the charm?

"Martha? You okay?" asked Mary. "It's not like you to daydream."

Martha snapped back to the present and took a deep breath to steady herself. "Sure. I'm all for the science fair. Count me in."

Brightly colored displays filled the auditorium of Conestoga Valley High School. The air buzzed with conversation and excitement. The sisters spent some time wandering from project to project until finally, Mary saw Alex from across the room. She waved at him, and he hurried over.

Mary made introductions. "Alex, these are my sisters, Elizabeth and Martha."

"Nice to meet you, ladies," Alex said. "Are you enjoying the fair so far?"

"We are," Elizabeth said. "It looks like you have a lot of bright students in this school. Some of these projects are quite impressive."

Martha had to agree. So far, she'd seen exhibits on computer algorithms, robotics, and artificial intelligence, to name only a few. Science fairs sure had come a long way since the days of light bulb potatoes and exploding volcanoes.

"I think we have some real talent hidden within these humble walls." Alex smiled warmly. "In fact, I was just talking to Mary about one of my most promising students. Cody Stephens. He's the one who took the drone footage at the balloon festival. Mary said you all are interested in talking to him?"

"We are," Martha said. Alex led them over to a large display in the corner of the room where a kid wearing a navy suit and striped tie stood out from a sea of more casually dressed teens. The trifold propped up on the table behind him featured a variety of complicated diagrams and a bunch of words Martha wasn't even sure how to pronounce.

"Are you judges?" asked Cody.

"No," Mary said. "We are interested in your project though."

"I'll let you all get acquainted," Alex said as he took a step away from their circle. "If you'll excuse me, I need to keep making the rounds with the other projects."

With his teacher gone, Cody's entire demeanor changed. His shoulders slumped, and he stared down toward his shoes.

Martha tried to draw him out. "Can you tell us some more about your project? Are these flies?" She reached closer to examine the poster board, which held ink drawings of the insects from all different angles.

"Not that it matters, but I built my own self-navigating drone based off the flight pattern of *Musca domestica*."

"The flight pattern of what?" Elizabeth asked. "I didn't quite catch that last part."

"*Musca domestica*," Cody answered slowly, as if they were hard of hearing. When they were still silent, he sighed loudly.

"You probably know it better as the common housefly." All Martha could think was that if this was how Cody treated adults, he'd be lucky if the real judges didn't boot him out of the fair posthaste. The kid was obviously intelligent, but he had a chip on his shoulder the size of a mountain.

Mary didn't seem to share Martha's irritation though. She looked at the boy as if she sympathized with him. She pulled Martha and Elizabeth aside for a minute. "Do you think you two could let me talk to him on my own? I know we're pretty easy to talk to, but even older ladies can be intimidating when they're running in a pack."

"Sure," Elizabeth said. "We'll visit some of the other displays, but before we leave, look over there."

Martha turned to gaze at a woman standing not far from them. She shook her head and looked at Elizabeth with a puzzled expression.

"What's wrong?" Mary asked.

"That's Deidre Ruble," Elizabeth whispered. "Our list goes down to one name."

One name. So the missing woman could be Kathryn McConnell?

Martha and Elizabeth stepped away from Cody's table. They were checking out the other displays when Elizabeth's phone rang. She reached into her purse and took it out. After walking away from the crowd, she answered.

"Hello?" she said.

Martha watched her as she listened to the voice on the other end of the line. "John," she mouthed to Martha. Then she turned her attention back to the call. "I don't know anyone with that name, but we'll certainly look into it. Thank you, John. I'll talk to you later."

She hung up and put her phone back in her purse. "Another missing person report. It's for someone in Reading. A Kathy Gimble." She frowned at Martha. "Do you know anyone with that name?"

Martha shook her head. "Sorry. But at least it's a lead."

She and Elizabeth had just gone back to looking at the science projects when Elizabeth stopped in her tracks. She stared at Martha with her mouth open.

"I just thought of something." She opened her purse and took out her phone again. After selecting a number, she waited for someone to answer. Martha moved closer so she could listen.

"John, it's Elizabeth. Is there any way you can find out what this Kathy Gimble's maiden name is?"

Martha watched as Elizabeth's eyes widened. "Can you come by the shop tomorrow? We need to talk." She paused, and then said. "Thanks." When she hung up, she turned to face Martha. "Kathy Gimble's maiden name is—"

"Don't tell me," Martha said, a feeling of excitement rising inside. "O'Connell?"

Elizabeth smiled. "John's coming by in the morning so we can find out more." She touched her sister's arm. "Maybe this is it, Martha. I think we've found her."

At that moment Martha heard a ping from her purse. She'd forwarded calls for the shop to her cell phone in hopes that someone might call them with information about the charm. She opened her purse and, after having some trouble finding it, her fingers finally closed around the phone.

"It's someone calling the shop. We sure are popular tonight."

"Do you recognize the number?" Elizabeth asked.

Martha glanced at the display. "No." She tapped the phone screen. "But I'm about to find out who it is. Hello?"

She held the phone to her ear, then pressed a finger over her other ear to block out the din from the science fair. A woman's raspy voice filled the phone.

"I know you probably don't remember me, but my name is Wanda Brewer. I work at the Two Bird Café. You were asking Myrtle about Darlene. Myrtle gave me the number for your shop. I'm not sure you'll get this tonight, but if you do, could you come by the restaurant? I need to talk to you."

There was a pause, and Martha could hear pots and pans clanging in the background. Wanda must be calling from the Two Bird now. The sounds were comforting and familiar, but the woman's next words, whispered furtively into the mouthpiece, were not. In fact, they made Martha's heart stall in her chest.

"I need to talk to you about Darlene. She may in trouble."

CHAPTER ELEVEN

Mary looked over Cody's project carefully, asking questions about it, trying to show him she was interested in what he'd accomplished. He answered her queries with short, flat responses. Mary sighed inwardly. This kid was going to be a tough nut to crack. She was getting ready to praise him for his efforts and move toward seeking the information she wanted from the night of the festival when several people stepped up to the display. Three men and three women. Each one dressed to the nines, their expressions serious and slightly disapproving. Who were they?

Mary started to speak to them, but Cody flashed her a look that stopped her in her tracks. She clamped her lips together and moved out of their way. She felt Cody would be happy if she would just leave him alone, but she had no intention of doing that. She was determined to find out if he had recorded something with his drone that might help them find the woman who had been accosted Friday night.

She jumped when someone grabbed her arm. It was Martha. "I got a call from a waitress at the Two Bird Café. She says she knows something about Darlene. She thinks she's in trouble. I'm not sure Darlene is the woman we're looking for, but we need to find out. We have to leave."

Mary glanced over at Cody. "I can't leave yet," she whispered. "You go on. I'll meet you there."

"But we're taking the car, Mary," Elizabeth said in a low voice. "How will you get to the restaurant?"

Mary scanned the room until her gaze settled on Alex. He was looking her way and smiled. She shook off a momentary twinge as she thought of seeing Bill in the store earlier.

"I can get a ride. I'll meet you as soon as I can." She waved at her sisters. "Get going. This might be what we've been waiting for. A really good lead."

Martha sighed. "All right. Just join us as quickly as possible." She glanced at her watch. "I don't think the Two Bird will be open much longer."

"I got it," Mary said with a smile. "Now scoot. We may still need to see this drone footage. We could learn something that might help us locate that poor woman."

Martha and Elizabeth hurried out the door, and Mary turned back to Cody's display and the people perusing it. All but one—a woman who looked none too happy with what she was seeing—were obviously judges. They were writing in small notebooks as they studied his display and whispered amongst themselves. Frankly, they looked like a group of sourpusses. Finally, one of the women addressed Cody.

"This is very well done, young man. You seem to have an extensive knowledge of drones."

Cody nodded and swallowed hard. It was clear to Mary that he was nervous. "I like the technology," he said, his voice a little shaky. "I feel drones will play a large part in our society in the future."

One of the men, older, with a carefully trimmed beard and a condescending expression, stepped closer to Cody. "Exactly what do you mean?"

Cody cleared his throat and threw back his shoulders. "Drones could be used for disaster aid. They can go places that are dangerous for rescuers. Finding survivors after a natural disaster—or even some kind of attack by terrorists—could not only save the lives of victims, but it could cut down on the risk to those sent to help them. Rather than a wide search, they could narrow their efforts to those the drones locate, helping both emergency personnel and the people who need assistance."

The judges were silent. Cody waited for a moment, but they didn't say anything, just made notes. After hearing his formal speech, Mary was marveling at the mixture of awkward teenager and prodigy that was standing in front of her.

"They could also be used to deliver supplies to people who need them," he continued. "Medicine, food, whatever is necessary for victims affected by disaster." Cody took a deep breath and let it out slowly. Although he was clearly nervous, Mary was impressed by his presentation. This young man had really thought this out. This was clearly his passion.

"They could also monitor wild animals," he said, "keeping environmentalists up to date on endangered species. And drones can be used to look over crime scenes, gather important information for law enforcement...and then of course there's the possibility of using them in the shipping industry."

The older man with the beard offered him a tight smile. "That's very interesting, young man. Very impressive display. Thank you."

The one woman who hadn't been conversing with the group stepped up to Cody's display and stared at his photographs. Some of them were from the balloon festival. She turned her attention to Mary. "I assume you're Cody's mother?" she asked.

Mary started to deny it, but the woman didn't give her the chance. "You might explain to your son that drones have been used to kill innocent people." Her tone was indignant. "Now it's much easier to murder people from a distance. Not a technology we need, in my opinion."

Cody's face turned red. "Attacking terrorists with drones stops them from killing innocent people, including our own citizens. They can protect our soldiers from harm."

"Ask the civilians who have died if they think drones are a good idea," the woman said. She shook her head as she addressed Mary. "You really need to have a talk with your son. He obviously doesn't have a grasp on reality." She turned to walk away.

"Excuse me," Mary said, trying to tamp down the anger she felt at the woman's reaction to Cody. "Your attitude is inappropriate. Cody sees drones as a way to help people. To rescue people. He believes we can assist those in need faster with drones—as well as protect people on the ground trying to perform rescues. For you to attack him because you have a problem with drones being used in war is unreasonable. He's not touting drones as weapons of war." Mary waved her hand over the display Cody had made. "Not one word about weapons of any kind. Trying to accuse him of something like that... It's just not fair."

The woman's eyes widened, and her cheeks turned crimson before she turned on her heel and hurried away.

The judge with the beard sighed. "I apologize for Stella. Her daughter is one of the contestants. She lost her son in Iraq a few years ago. It had nothing to do with drones, but her grief has turned her against all things military." He smiled at Cody. "Your display is exceptional. Don't let her comments upset you." He turned to Mary. "You're obviously a great mother. This is an extraordinary young man. Congratulations."

Before Mary could correct him, the group moved toward the next display. Cody turned away from Mary and began straightening the pictures on the poster board.

"I would have told them I'm not your mother," Mary said, "but they left before I could. I'm sorry. Do you want me to follow them and clear that up?"

When Cody turned around, Mary was struck by the hurt she saw in his eyes.

"I'm sorry, Cody," she said. "That was unfair. Your project is really well done."

"It's not that," he said. "My parents…"

Although he didn't finish his thought, Mary was pretty sure she knew what he was thinking. Why weren't his parents here? Why would the judges mistake her for his mother? Mary scanned the room. It looked to her like most of the other students had family around them. In contrast, Cody had only Mary with him.

"I hope you don't mind my asking," Mary asked, "but where are your parents, Cody?"

Cody's expression hardened. "They're busy with their jobs. My father's an engineer, and my mother runs a nonprofit organization. They don't have time for frivolous things like this science fair."

Cody pulled a box out from under the skirted table that held his display and began to disassemble his project.

"What are you doing?" Mary asked. "The fair isn't over yet."

"It is for me," Cody said, his tone sharp. "Thanks to what that woman said to the judges, there's no chance I'm going to win. I'm going home."

"Cody, please don't do this," Mary said, trying to keep her voice down so no one else would hear her. "You should leave your display up until the fair is over. No one else is taking theirs down. Please wait until after the judging."

"You're not my mother," he snapped. "You can't tell me what to do."

"I know that, but please, just listen to me."

Cody stopped his efforts to dismantle his display. He sighed and put it back together. "Okay, okay." When he finished getting everything back in place, he turned to her. "Why are you here?" he asked. "What do you want?"

"Didn't Mr. Wright explain about the balloon festival footage?"

Cody frowned. "He started to tell me something about that, but then he got called over by another kid who needed help with his project."

Mary had hoped Alex would have paved the way for her, but that hadn't happened. She quickly explained what Martha had seen the night of the festival. "We think your drone might have captured something that will help us discover the identity of the kidnapped woman."

Cody granted her the first smile she'd seen from him. "See, I told you. Drones can be used to help law enforcement. I can help you go through the footage with Mr. Wright."

Mary was touched by his willingness to help. She had achieved her objective and wondered if she should talk to Alex now about a ride, but she just couldn't leave yet. Cody shouldn't be alone. Whether he won or lost, he needed someone by his side. As they waited, Mary sensed that he was grateful she was there, but he didn't say it.

A few minutes later, a woman's voice came through the PA system, announcing that the judges were ready to reveal the winner of the science fair. Mary turned around and saw the man with the beard standing at the front of the room, a microphone next to him. The room fell silent as everyone waited for him to speak. Mary held her breath, hoping Cody would win.

The man cleared his throat and then said, "For his impressive project, the winner of the science fair is Cody Stephens."

Mary was excited and happy, although she couldn't help but feel some anger toward Cody's parents. They should be here for this. Alex came over to congratulate Cody. He was clearly proud of his student.

Cody accepted the award and congratulations from all of the judges. Stella wasn't anywhere to be found. Mary wasn't angry with the woman anymore. She couldn't begin to understand the pain of losing a child. Just thinking about it brought tears to her eyes. Mary purposed in her heart to pray for the distraught mother.

While Cody was being congratulated for his win, Mary pulled Alex aside and asked him for a ride to the Two Bird Café. He agreed, telling her that first he needed to greet some of the parents who'd shown up. He assured her he wouldn't be long.

As Mary waited, she wondered what Martha and Elizabeth were finding out from the waitress at the café. Would she help them find the missing woman? As the days ticked past, Mary worried that the danger was growing for the victim. She looked over at Cody. Was he right? Was his drone capable of helping catch a criminal?

She'd find out soon.

CHAPTER TWELVE

Martha's stomach grumbled as she entered the Two Bird Café. She'd made herself a turkey sandwich for dinner, but the meal had apparently not stuck with her very long. While it felt a little indulgent to be ordering something to eat at such a late hour, it was better than listening to her stomach rumble while she was talking to Wanda.

Martha slipped into a booth, and Elizabeth sat down opposite her.

"I'm going to order something," said Elizabeth, and Martha couldn't help but laugh.

"You read my mind."

"I wonder how things are going with Mary. Cody sure seemed to have a chip on his shoulder."

"Mary knows more about his situation than I do," Martha said. "I don't think she would have stayed behind unless she really thought it was necessary. I hope she talked him into letting us see the drone footage. It could be important." She sighed. "I wonder what Wanda wants to tell us."

As if on cue, Wanda approached their table. "Can I get you ladies something to drink?"

Elizabeth ordered a berry-infused tea, and Martha asked for a decaf coffee. Wanda took their orders to the kitchen, then after some time, returned to the table again to get their food orders. Martha wondered when Wanda was going to divulge the information she'd seemed so insistent about over the phone.

"What did you want to tell us about Darlene?" she blurted out.

"I'm sorry," Wanda said. "We've really gotten slammed."

A large man stepped out of the kitchen and glared at Wanda. "Your orders are piling up. Quit talking and get to work!"

Wanda's face turned red. "That's my boss, Hal. The café closes in thirty minutes." She lowered her voice. "I'll meet you outside after my shift is done." She hurried back to the kitchen to fetch the orders waiting for her.

After a few minutes, Wanda brought their food to the table. Martha didn't even taste her club sandwich as she ate. All she could do was stare at the red-and-white enamel clock hanging on the wall and count down the minutes until the diner closed. What did Wanda want to tell them? Did it have anything to do with the missing woman?

After what seemed like an eternity, someone turned off the fluorescent OPEN sign in the front window, and a busboy started mopping the floors. Martha and Elizabeth carefully maneuvered around the slippery patches and went to the front register to pay. Wanda was nowhere to be seen, but they headed out into the parking lot anyway, just as Mary pulled up in Alex's vehicle. She hopped out and waved cheerily at him. He waved back before driving away.

"How was the fair?" Elizabeth asked Mary as she walked up to them.

"Very interesting. I have a lot to tell you. What's going on here?"

Martha sighed. "Not sure. We're waiting to talk to Wanda."

The diner's interior lights flicked off, one by one. "They're closed now," Martha said. "So where is she?"

"I don't see anyone," Elizabeth said. Not that there had been much of a crowd anyway, as late as they'd been, but the few people who'd been sitting at tables earlier had cleared out.

"There she is," Mary said. Wanda approached them from the back of the café.

"Listen, I don't want to spread gossip," she said when she reached them. "Goodness knows, enough of that gets spread around in there without me adding to it. But Darlene and I are friends. The night of the balloon festival, we were both working the dinner shift together. She'd acted normal all afternoon, but then all of a sudden, I ran into her after leaving the kitchen with an order, and she was—out of sorts."

"Out of sorts? How do you mean?" Elizabeth asked.

"She was worried. Nervous. That wasn't like Darlene. She usually has a good head on her shoulders, very no-nonsense." Wanda heaved a sigh. It was obvious she really was worried about her friend. "When I asked her what was wrong, she wouldn't tell me. The only thing she would say was that she'd overheard something she shouldn't have. Then the next day, she was gone. She called Hal and told him she had to have some time off to take care of her sister who'd gotten sick suddenly. I didn't even know she had a sister. She never talked about her."

Elizabeth latched on to Wanda's words. "You said Darlene heard something she shouldn't have. What do you think that means?"

"Oh goodness, I don't know. I've been turning it over in my mind since she told me. The only thing I can think is that she overheard some conversation in the café that was confidential. Lots of people use the café as a meeting place."

"Can you think of anyone who was in the restaurant that night who seemed suspicious?"

Wanda looked thoughtful. "I'd have to go back through receipts to know for sure, but we weren't very busy that night. If I'm right I only had three tables. I do remember that Dan Feinstein was there." She frowned. "He's been in several times having cozy conversations with a nice-looking older woman."

"What's wrong with that?" Mary asked, her cheeks pink. Martha wondered if she was thinking about Alex and the time they'd been spending together.

"The woman's not his wife," Wanda said flatly. "Dan's been married to Gayla for a lot of years, but this woman isn't Gayla. Her name's Maddie."

"I see. Anyone else you can think of?" Elizabeth asked.

Wanda chewed her lip. "Well, there's another man who's been stopping in for dinner a few times a week. He might have been there. I think he's a lawyer. Always dressed to the nines in a suit and tie, carrying a briefcase. He's been meeting with a lady who's jumpier than a jackrabbit. Every time I set the coffeepot down, she startles."

"Hmm," Martha said, trying to reset her thoughts. She'd been certain Wanda was going to talk about Kathy. "Can you think of anybody else who might have upset Darlene?" A lawyer could certainly be discussing confidential information with a client, but they didn't usually get important cases in Bird-in-Hand. Not serious enough, she'd imagine, to warrant kidnapping someone. The man who might be cheating on his wife was a possibility though. Crimes of passion had driven any number of people to act out of character.

"Well, there is this guy she dated a couple of times. He's been hanging around a lot. A really unsavory character. When she first went out with him he seemed fine, but then he started asking her for money, and she broke it off. I don't trust him."

"Do you know his name?"

Wanda sighed. "I think his name is Arnold, but I don't know his last name."

"Do you think we could get some names from you after you check the receipts?"

"Sure," Wanda said. "I'll take a look at them tomorrow and give you a call. Listen, maybe I'm being paranoid, but I know you all are looking for a missing woman, and Darlene is missing. At least, as far as I'm concerned. I've tried to call her, but she has one of those cell phones where you to have to buy minutes. She's always forgetting to do that. Every time I've called, it's gone straight to voice mail. I don't want to be suspicious. I just want to make sure she's okay."

Mary patted Wanda's arm soothingly. "I don't think you're being suspicious. You just care about your friend. We'll do everything we can to find out where she is and if she's okay."

"I appreciate it," Wanda said with tears shining in her eyes. "I'd like to think she'd watch out for me the same way."

Martha, Mary, and Elizabeth waited in the parking lot, making sure Wanda got to her car safely. As they stood there,

Mary said, "I'm confused. I thought Wanda had information about Kathy Gimble. Now it seems we have two missing women."

"We'll talk to John in the morning about Kathy," Elizabeth said. She sighed loudly. "You're right. Now we have two possibilities."

"I guess that's better than none at all," Mary said.

Martha's mind was still spinning with questions when she saw movement outside of the café. A man wearing a knit cap skulked along the side of the building, sticking to the shadows as though trying to conceal his presence. Martha held her breath, but Wanda soon appeared, safe and sound, behind the wheel of her car. She honked a goodbye at them as she turned out of the parking lot onto the street. The man had disappeared.

"Who was that?" Mary asked in a hushed tone.

"I have no idea," Martha said. "Let's get out of here."

"I agree," Elizabeth said. "We can talk about this more at home."

As Martha headed to her car, her thoughts were confused. She couldn't tell what was a clue and what wasn't anymore. Two missing women. Both of them on their list. Which one was the woman they were looking for? And who was that man skulking around the restaurant? Was he just a pedestrian, cutting through the lot on his way to another location? Or could he have something to do with a missing woman?

CHAPTER THIRTEEN

Martha and Mary sat at the kitchen table, waiting for Elizabeth to heat up water for tea.

"So what do you think?" Martha asked her sisters. "Which woman is the one we're searching for?"

"I have no idea," Mary said. "Until we hear from John, we can't zero in on one person."

"Wanda's information was really compelling," Elizabeth said. "I mean, if Darlene doesn't have a sister…"

Martha groaned. "That's the problem. Wanda isn't sure if she does or not. Until we know for sure, we can't assume she's our victim."

Elizabeth handed Martha and Mary cups of hot water and tea bags. Then she poured water into her own cup and draped her own tea bag over the side. She sat down at the table. "Darlene obviously overheard something that upset her. Whether or not she's the woman you saw, Martha, I think something's really wrong there."

Martha sighed. "I do too." Her gaze swung between her sisters. "So what do we do now?"

"We talk to John. Let's find out what he has to say about Kathryn…I mean Kathy," Elizabeth said.

Martha frowned. "I don't remember her. I've tried and tried. Gone over everyone I knew at camp."

Mary cleared her throat. "I…I knew her. I went to school with her, and we were in Scouts together. You knew her too, Martha. And you met her, Elizabeth. She was my age. That's why you didn't recall her."

"Why didn't you say something before now?" Elizabeth asked.

Mary shook her head. "I knew her as Kathy. I didn't remember her last name. I'm sorry. I wasn't thinking. I should have realized…"

"That's okay," Martha said. "We were confused about it too for a while." She smiled at her sister, hoping to make her feel better.

"Well," Mary said, "I didn't know her well, but she was a nice girl. Very quiet. She was in my tent. She and I wrote a play we put on for the camp. Each tent had to perform. I remember Kathy was really bright and creative. The truth is, she wrote the play. I had very little to do with it. It was very well received when we put it on." She stopped and looked off into the distance, obviously trying to remember something. "It was about a bunny. I think his name was…"

"Never mind," Martha said. "Did you see her after that?"

Mary shook her head. "She told me her parents were getting a divorce and she and her mother were moving to Reading. Of course, that meant she was going to a different school."

"So she's gone missing," Elizabeth said softly. "I wonder why."

"I hope John has the answer to that question," Mary said. "What time is he coming by tomorrow?"

Elizabeth shrugged. "He just said he'd be by in the morning."

Martha sighed. "So it's either Kathy Gimble or Darlene. I think Kathy is the most likely. Just because Wanda doesn't know if Darlene has a sister... Well, it's not enough to convince me she's the woman I saw abducted."

"I think you're right," Mary said. "Kathy is our missing woman."

"I'm not so sure," Elizabeth said slowly.

"Why do you say that?" Martha asked. She was certain they were finally on the right track. Elizabeth's comment puzzled her. They didn't need to get sidetracked. Kathy needed them.

Elizabeth took a sip of her tea, her expression troubled. "I keep thinking about the way Darlene acted. Something upset her, and now she's gone?"

"But she called in, Lizzie," Martha said, trying to stay calm. "That means she really did take off on her own. She couldn't be the woman we're looking for."

"Unless someone forced her to place that phone call," Mary said. "I agree with Elizabeth. We need to keep Darlene on our list."

Martha finished her tea and stood. "I still think Kathy Gimble is it. She went to the camp. She had a charm. And she's missing. I don't think it could be any clearer. But maybe after we talk to John, we'll know for sure." She rubbed her forehead. "I'm getting a headache."

"I didn't mean to upset you," Elizabeth said. "I was just..."

Martha waved her comment away. "You didn't do anything wrong. I'm just tired...and worried."

"You're doing everything you can," Elizabeth said gently. "I'm proud of you, Martha. You could have ignored what you saw. I believe we're going to find that woman, and it will be because you didn't give up."

Tears sprang to Martha's eyes. "Thanks, Lizzie. That means a lot." She looked over at her younger sister. "And you too, Mary. I'm so glad I have my sisters in my life. I don't know what I'd do without you."

"The feeling is absolutely mutual," Mary said with a smile.

Martha felt her emotions building again. She just mumbled "Good night," and headed for the stairs. She'd slept fitfully ever since the balloon festival. When she closed her eyes, all she could see was the woman looking up at her, probably hoping Martha would rescue her. If only she'd been able to actually see the woman clearly, the search would be much easier. As she got ready for bed, Martha prayed that John would bring them information that would finally point them in the right direction.

The sisters woke to a rainy morning. The rain came in sheets, with thunder announcing each wave. When they opened the shop, only a handful of people showed up. Martha kept watching the doors. Where was John? Finally, around eleven o'clock, the doors slid open, and John came in. Mary hurried up to the front of the store where Elizabeth and Martha already waited. He smiled when he saw the three of them staring at him. There were no customers in the store, and Martha hoped no one would come in. She wanted to hear what John had to say.

He held up his hand. "I know you're all eager to know about Kathy Gimble, but I don't have any other information except that she's missing."

"Who filed the report?" Martha asked.

John pulled a stool over and sat down. "Her husband. Kathy was supposed to be visiting her mother in Paradise. He assumed she was there, but when he talked to Mrs. O'Connell, she told him she hadn't seen Kathy. She'd just assumed she couldn't come."

"When was she supposed to show up?" Martha asked.

"Friday night. And she told her husband she was going to stop by the balloon festival on her way out of town."

"So she would have been there at the right time," Elizabeth said.

"She's missing, she was at the festival, and she had a charm from the camp," Martha said.

"Before you get too excited, I asked her husband, Devin, about the charm. He didn't know anything about it. Said she'd mentioned it years ago, but she didn't know where it was."

"That conversation was a long time ago," Martha said. "She could have found it by now. She has to be our missing woman. Now we just need to find her."

John held his hand up. "Not sure what you mean by 'we.' I'll be the one looking for her. You're not law enforcement. Just relax and let me do my job. If Kathy was abducted, the man who did it is dangerous."

John stood up and headed toward the door, but before he left, he turned around. "I'll keep you updated, but I meant what I said. Mind your own business, okay? I don't want any of you getting hurt."

Although Martha nodded along with her sisters, she was determined to find Kathy Gimble.

As if reading her mind, Elizabeth said, "We need to listen to John, Martha. Putting ourselves in danger isn't going to help Kathy...or whoever that woman turns out to be."

"Whoever she turns out to be?" Martha said. "Didn't you hear John? It has to be Kathy."

"Maybe, but until we know for sure, I want us all to follow John's advice and stay out of his way."

Although Martha didn't say anything in response to Elizabeth's warning, she had no intention of backing off until Kathy was home safe.

CHAPTER FOURTEEN

Martha busied herself cleaning up the store, trying not to worry about Kathy Gimble. Where could she be? She was restocking the bakery shelves when her phone rang. She took it out of the pocket of her apron and checked the name of the caller before answering. Wanda.

"I'm sorry it took me so long to call you," Wanda said. "I had to be careful and not let Hal see what I was doing. Since the receipts were already filed, it would look suspicious if he caught me going through them."

"Maybe you should tell him what's going on," Martha said. "Darlene has worked at the café a long time. He might be concerned about her too."

Wanda paused a moment before saying, "I don't know. I've worked with him for several years. He's not the kind of person you get close to, you know? He's our boss, but that's it. Besides, what if Darlene just said she was at her sister's but she's really somewhere else? I don't want to get her in trouble."

Wanda didn't sound as concerned about Darlene as she had when she first contacted them. That was normal. People usually began to question themselves after they had time to reevaluate their suspicions, especially when it came to someone being in danger.

"Hal would be angry if he found out I gave you information about our customers without proof that Darlene had really been abducted," Wanda continued.

Even though Martha was now convinced Kathy was the woman she saw Friday night, she couldn't just ignore clues. Following up with Wanda was the smart thing to do. Just in case. "I understand, and I appreciate your effort. We have no intention of telling Hal about the receipts, don't worry. So what did you find out?"

"Besides Dan Feinstein, the only other receipt was for someone with the name of D. Carlton. I think he might have been the lawyer. The other table must have paid cash. And by the way, there's something I should have remembered when we talked. I don't know why I didn't. I guess I was trying so hard to recall anything unusual that happened that night, it just slipped my mind. Besides, I don't usually pay that much attention to people. Getting their food out on time is my main focus."

"Of course," Martha said. "What else did you recall?"

"It's about Dan Feinstein. I told you he was having supper with a woman who wasn't his wife. Anyway, at one point I saw Dan hand something to Darlene. At the time, I didn't think much about it. I figured it was a tip—or maybe he was paying his bill. But then I remembered that they had just gotten their food. Besides, I saw him at the counter paying for their meal before he left, so it couldn't have been his check." She grunted. "That woman he was with left before he did. Trying to hide the fact that they were together, if you ask me."

"So what do you think he gave Darlene?" Martha asked, trying to get Wanda back to the subject at hand.

"It looked like a note."

"A note?"

"Yeah. I mean, I'm just guessing, but I think I'm right. Listen, I'd better get back to work now, or Hal will have my head."

"One other thing, Wanda," Martha said, taking a deep breath. "Look, I know this is a long shot, but do you know anything about a charm Darlene won at Girl Scout camp when she was a girl? It was for..."

"Being helpful?" Wanda asked, interrupting her.

Martha felt the hair on the back of her neck stand up. "Yes. How do you know about that?"

Wanda's laugh came through the phone. "She loved her scouting days. Wears that bracelet all the time."

Martha thanked Wanda and hung up. Then she turned to her sisters who were standing nearby, waiting to hear what Wanda had said.

"I've changed my mind," Martha said, breathlessly. "It's Darlene. She's definitely our missing woman."

"How do you know that, Martha?" Elizabeth asked. "You were convinced it was Kathy."

"Well, of course, we can't be absolutely certain," Martha said. "All we can do is to make an educated guess, but I think I'm right."

"Why? What did Wanda say?" Elizabeth asked.

"Well, first of all, she remembered something very interesting."

"What's that?" Mary asked.

"She saw Dan Feinstein pass a note to Darlene. Now that sounds pretty suspicious."

"I hate the idea of talking to Dan," Elizabeth said. "I mean, we've been to their gift shop many times. He and Gayla are so sweet. I just can't imagine him having an affair."

"I know," Martha said, "but we'll have to ask him some questions, Elizabeth. We owe it to Darlene."

"If Darlene is really missing," Mary said.

"Of course. Now, let me tell you why I'm convinced Darlene is the one we're looking for." She moved closer to her sisters as if someone was in the shop even though they were alone. "Darlene wore a charm bracelet. Every day. And one of the charms was…"

"The Girl Scout award for being helpful?" Mary asked, excitement in her voice.

This was the second time someone had interrupted her when she was ready to mention the charm. "Yes. Kathy's husband said she had no idea where her charm was. But Darlene wore a bracelet with all the charms she won at camp."

"But what if she's really at her sister's?" Elizabeth asked.

"If she actually has a sister," Martha said, shaking her head. "Remember what Mary said last night. Maybe the kidnapper forced her to call."

Elizabeth snapped her fingers. "And she gave the excuse about a sister as a clue. So Wanda would realize that something was wrong. That Darlene needed help."

"First of all, we have to find out if she even has a sister," Martha said, a note of frustration in her voice. "How can we find out for sure?"

"We need to ask Wanda if she knows any of Darlene's other relatives," Mary said. "Her mother, father… Anyone who could confirm if there's a sister. Hopefully, Wanda can steer us in the right direction. She's the only person we know who has a close relationship with Darlene. If we find out Darlene doesn't have a sister, then with all the other evidence, we'll know we're on the right track."

"I think that's a great idea," Martha said.

"Can you call her now?" Elizabeth asked.

Martha frowned. "I'd hate to. She was in a rush. It's almost noon. I'm sure this is one of her busiest times."

"Well, since we're closing today at two, maybe we should run over to the restaurant and have a late lunch," Mary said.

"I don't know," Elizabeth said. "We were just there last night. We don't want to put Wanda under too much pressure. She's already tried to help us by going through the receipts."

"I don't think there's anything wrong with it," Martha said. "We need to get some solid evidence to give to John. As long as no one files a missing person report for Darlene he can't really do anything."

At that moment someone walked in the front door, carrying a box. It was a local woman, Lillian Carstairs. She was moving from her large family house to a smaller apartment. Secondhand Blessings was a good place to take items someone didn't want to keep, especially if they weren't interested in an estate sale. Lillian had said she didn't want to mess with people traipsing through her house, staring at her possessions, so she'd asked the sisters to help her. Elizabeth went to meet her and collect the box.

"I hope there's something in here you can use," Lillian said, plopping the box down on the front counter. She was a small woman with tightly curled hair dyed dark gray but with a definite blue tone. She was the perfect caricature of a little old blue-haired lady. And although Lillian was elderly, she was still full of vim and vigor. She spoke her mind and didn't suffer fools gladly.

"I'm sure we can find a place for most of it," Elizabeth told her. She started removing items from the box. The first thing was a lovely music box.

Lillian reached over and rested her hand on it gently. "My Raymond bought that for me on our first anniversary," she said in a soft voice.

"Maybe you should keep it," Elizabeth said.

Lillian stepped back from the box and straightened her shoulders. "No, I have some other things he gave me. I can't keep them all. He's been gone five years now. If he were still here, he'd be saying, 'Now, Lilly, you get rid of all this stuff and get yourself a smaller place where you'll be happy.'" Her eyes turned shiny, but she quickly blinked away the tears. The no-nonsense Lillian was back.

"You can go through the rest of this later," she said. "Just let me know what you can use and what you can't."

With that, she turned and left through the sliding doors.

Martha came over to the counter and looked at the music box. It was beautiful. Carved wood. When opened, it played "The Anniversary Waltz" while a small red bird danced around in a circle. She slowly closed the lid and wiped away the tears that had slid down her cheeks. Chuck had been gone a while now, but sometimes, like now, it felt as if he'd died yesterday.

Elizabeth, who obviously sensed what Martha was feeling, came around the counter and put her arm around her, and Martha leaned into her.

"Chuck and I loved that song," she said, her voice quaking. She shook her head and gave Elizabeth a hug. "Thanks, Lizzie," she said. "I'm okay."

"Good. Now, let's finish up our day and head over to the Two Bird," Elizabeth said softly. "We need to find out about Darlene's relatives."

Martha smiled. "Sounds good." She knew Elizabeth was trying to distract her, and she appreciated it. Time to put her mind on the task at hand. They needed to find out if Darlene had a sister. Maybe the truth would confirm that they should be looking for Darlene. Still, she worried about Kathy. Where was she? Although she'd tried to convince her sisters that Darlene was the person they were looking for, Martha couldn't get her mind off Kathy.

CHAPTER FIFTEEN

I might have to leave for lunch a bit early," Mary said. "I promised Alex and Cody that I'd meet up with them today. Cody agreed to show me the video footage he has from the balloon festival."

"I'd almost forgotten about the drone footage," Elizabeth said. "Good job, Mary."

Mary dropped a pretend curtsy. "I do my best."

"All right." Martha clapped her hands together. Finally, she felt they were making some progress. They were going to check with Wanda about Darlene's relatives, and Mary was looking at footage taken by Cody's drone on Friday night. Surely something would finally lead them in the right direction. She wondered what John was learning but figured he'd call them if he had any information.

The sisters finished closing up shop and headed outside to climb into Martha's car. "What about Dan Feinstein?" Martha asked. "Are we going to try to talk to him today?"

"I don't know," Elizabeth said. "I feel so odd about confronting him. We don't have a shred of evidence other than idle gossip, which I'm not inclined to put much stock in."

"If only we knew what was written in that note that he gave Darlene," Mary said.

"Maybe it was a warning," Martha suggested. She started the car, and as if on cue, an icon flashed up on her dashboard. That silly light again. She still hadn't taken her car in to get the oil changed, but she wasn't too far over the recommended mileage. Surely it would be all right. She just didn't have time to deal with vehicle maintenance right now. Not when a woman's life was in jeopardy and they were getting so close to figuring everything out.

"Hmm." Mary looked thoughtful. "You've got a point, Martha. It's possible the note was a warning. That would explain why Darlene got so upset afterward. I suppose it would be a bit much to dumpster dive through the trash behind the Two Bird?"

Martha couldn't help but laugh as she imagined the sisters up to their necks in rotting banana peels and broken eggshells. Not a likely scenario, though she knew they'd done some unorthodox things before in the name of solving a mystery. Maybe they'd table that for a worst-case scenario. She headed toward the café. "Now that you mention dumpster diving, talking to Dan doesn't seem too bad in comparison."

Elizabeth offered a solution. "Maybe if we just go to his shop and talk with him and Gayla, something will come up in conversation. It's possible that this whole thing is just a misunderstanding. Do you think we should go there first?"

"I'm starving," Mary said. "Let's get something to eat now. Then you and Martha can visit the Feinsteins while I see Cody at the school. We can meet up at home this evening to compare notes."

"Sounds like a plan," Elizabeth said.

Before long they reached the Two Bird Café. Martha hurried to a back-corner booth and slid into the side facing the front door. That way, it would be easy to keep an eye on the customers who came in and out of the restaurant. Hopefully, they could see at least one of the people Wanda had mentioned in her earlier conversation. Elizabeth and Mary sat down opposite Martha. Wanda raised her eyebrows as she approached their table. "Back so soon?"

Martha glanced around to see if anyone was in earshot of their conversation. The last thing she wanted to do was get Wanda in hot water with her boss, but locating a woman in trouble was more important. She kept her voice soft as she addressed Wanda. "You mentioned earlier that you didn't know if Darlene had a sister. What about other relatives? Anyone who lives in the area?"

Wanda leaned close over the table and spoke in a low voice. "Darlene's father lives down the road from her house. You can look her up in the phone book, and her father—Clyde's his name—is two houses down on the same side of the street. If he asks you who sent you, don't mention my name, okay?" Wanda straightened to her full height and raised her voice to a normal volume. "Now, what can I get you ladies to drink?"

The rest of the meal passed uneventfully, though Martha kept her eyes glued to the front door in hopes a person of interest might appear. Mary finished up the last few bites of her sourdough BLT and stood. "I need to head out. I can't wait to hear what you find out at the Feinsteins'."

Elizabeth sighed. "If we discover anything. I still feel odd approaching them, especially if Dan and Gayla are having marriage troubles. It really isn't our place to get involved."

"We're not getting involved," Martha assured her. "We're just—" She searched her mind for the right words. "Okay, maybe we are getting involved. But it's all for a good reason. What if Dan had something to do with Darlene's disappearance? A little meddling could save an innocent woman's life."

Elizabeth gulped down the last of her coffee. "All right. I want to tread cautiously though."

"Agreed," Martha said.

Mary left a generous tip on the table for Wanda. "See you guys later." She took off as Martha and Elizabeth went to the register to pay, and then they left too. As Martha started her car engine, Elizabeth peered over her shoulder at the dashboard.

"Is that light still on?" she asked.

Martha heaved a sigh. "Yes, and I'm planning to take care of it soon. I just haven't had time."

"All right." Elizabeth pressed her lips together and didn't say anything else.

Martha was thankful. She'd take care of the car eventually. There were just more pressing matters at hand right now. Like figuring out if Dan Feinstein was a kidnapper.

She pulled into the large gravel lot in front of Feinstein's Fine Gifts & More. Gayla had a talent for creating decorative displays, and this month was no exception. September's focus was apple-based products, and Gayla had adorned the porch with metal washtubs overflowing with apples of varying colors.

The windows were filled with cookbooks and artfully arranged jars of apple butter tied with plaid bows.

A tiny bell announced their entry at the front door. Dan and Gayla were busy tidying a display of old-fashioned stick candy, but Dan immediately looked up and waved them inside. "Well, if it isn't the Classen sisters."

Martha was surprised he remembered them, as they didn't visit the store frequently. Of course, some people just never forgot a face.

"Come in, come in. Would you all like some fresh-pressed apple cider?" Dan walked to a table set up by the register and poured two cups full. "Made it this morning. We recently bought a press and got set up to make and bottle our own cider on the premises. It's been something we've wanted to do for a long time. We get the apples from the Hennessey orchard. It's a great partnership." He seemed so joyful over such a simple thing that Martha felt a twinge of guilt. It might be more difficult to confront Dan than she'd imagined.

She accepted the small paper cup of cider Dan handed her. "Thank you."

Elizabeth took a sip from her cup. "This is delicious."

"I don't think it's bad for a first try," Dan said. "We have more plans for expansion in the future. Gayla is a gem at coming up with innovative ideas. She's kept us going since we opened."

"Oh, you." Gayla swatted playfully at Dan. "You've put in a lot of hard work too, as I recall."

Dan continued. "We've been contacting local restaurants to see if they'd like to carry our cider. Gayla made some great fliers, and I've been passing them out."

"Did you think about the Two Bird Café?" Martha asked. She had a feeling she knew what the note that Dan had passed to Darlene was the night she disappeared.

"Yes. In fact, I was just there Friday night. I gave a flier to the waitress to pass along to the owner."

Martha and Elizabeth exchanged a look, and Elizabeth quickly changed the subject.

"How long have you all owned the store?" she asked.

"Well, let's see." Dan scratched his chin. "We started the store two years after we got married, and we're celebrating twenty-three years this month, so...twenty-one years. Hard to believe it's been that long."

"Time flies when you're having fun." Gayla smiled.

"And when you enjoy the people you're with every day." Dan put his arm around his wife's shoulders and squeezed her in an affectionate hug. She seemed equally smitten and reached up to plant a kiss on his cheek. Either this guy was the real deal or a real coldhearted cheater.

"Congratulations on your anniversary and on the success of the store," Elizabeth said. "Is it mainly you two who work here?"

"Mostly. We do have a new addition to the staff recently," Dan said. "Gayla's adopted, but she recently reconnected with her biological mother. She's going to be helping out at the store some through the week." He called into the back room. "Madelyn? Are you back there?"

"I'm here."

Martha heard a rustling in the back room, then a striking older woman with dark hair and coloring similar to Gayla's rounded the corner.

"You needed something?"

"I just wanted to introduce you to the Classen sisters. Minus one, if my memory serves me?"

Elizabeth smiled. "Mary is busy today."

"Mary, that's right." Dan turned to the dark-haired woman beside him. "Well, I'm pleased to introduce you to two-thirds of the Classen clan."

The woman extended her hand to greet Martha and Elizabeth. "Hi, I'm Madelyn. But please call me Maddie."

CHAPTER SIXTEEN

It was still raining when Mary arrived at the school. She kept an umbrella in her car just for occasions like this. She reached behind her on the floor and grabbed it. Then she got her purse and opened the car door. After pushing the button on the umbrella, she held it over her head as she got out. Once she reached the entrance of the school, she checked in with a security guard before being allowed to go to the main office, where she sat down and waited for Alex to come and get her. There were three young students sitting near her and none of them looked happy. A door opened, and a man stood there. He was rather imposing, and Mary noticed that the teenage girl sitting next to her suddenly straightened up in her chair. The man, who had to be the principal, beckoned to the girl.

"Back again, Miss Abrams?" he asked.

The girl stood up, tossed back a mane of blond hair, and marched bravely toward his office, where another woman waited. Maybe Miss Abrams's teacher? It didn't look too good for the girl. Before she entered the office, she looked back for some reason. Mary gave her a reassuring smile. Surprisingly, the girl smiled back, then turned to face her judgment.

Mary couldn't help but remember when she'd been in the girl's place. She hadn't been a troublemaker in school, but she'd had problems being quiet in class. She'd been sent to the principal's office several times by teachers who couldn't get her to pay attention. Their principal, Miss Curtis, was always gentle with her. She would explain why it was important to let the teacher talk, but frankly, Mary got the impression Miss Curtis thought the whole thing was rather funny. Memories of Miss Curtis made her a little emotional, and she had to pull a tissue out of her purse to wipe her eyes. She had just put it back when the door next to her opened and Alex came into the room.

"Sorry I'm a little late," he said with a smile. "Kids in my classroom don't always work with my schedule."

Mary stood up. "I completely understand. I'm so glad Cody's willing to let me see the footage from Friday night."

Alex held the door open and ushered Mary into the hallway. "I hope we have something you can use," he said as he started down the hall. Mary followed him, unsure where they were going.

"Have you looked at the footage?" she asked as they turned a corner and headed down a different hallway.

"No, sorry. Just too busy." He pointed up at a large clock on the wall. "Classes are just getting ready to change. I don't have anything this period, and Cody has study hall. That's why I felt this would be the perfect time for us to—"

A loud bell sounded, and Mary jumped. It was so noisy it drowned out Alex's next words. Doors swung open, and students streamed out into the hallway. Alex put his hand on Mary's shoulder and helped her weave her way through the crush of bodies on their way to their next class.

They finally stopped, and Alex opened a door where a few teenagers were still working on papers.

"I said to finish those by the end of the period," Alex said to them. "Up here, now." He pointed at a desk at the front of the room. The students stood, a couple of them with rather worried expressions. They put their books in their backpacks and took the papers they'd been working on up to Alex's desk. After they left, Alex chuckled. "That group likes to visit. That's why they don't get their assignments done on time unless I'm in the room with them." He grinned at Mary. "I expect you understand them rather well."

"I was thinking about that while I waited outside the principal's office. So you remember how I used to get in trouble for talking?"

"Of course I do. I remember a lot of things about you. I had a crush on you, but I was too afraid to tell you."

Mary looked at him in surprise. "You should have said something."

He shrugged. "Yeah, I should have. But I'm glad we've reconnected." He shook his head. "You know, I miss that old school building."

"Me too," Mary said. "But this new school is very nice. Much bigger and more modern. I guess progress marches on."

"I guess it does." Alex pointed toward a back table with chairs. "Let's sit back there. Cody should arrive any minute."

As if Cody had heard his name, he opened the classroom door and came in. Mary greeted him with a smile.

"Thank you so much for doing this, Cody," she said. "Have you found anything that might help us?"

He came over and sat down. He removed a laptop from a case he carried and put it on the table. "Maybe. I hope so." He opened the laptop, turned it on, and then clicked the keys until a video popped up. He advanced the video to one particular spot. "I think I was filming the balloon you were in. Is this it?"

Mary looked closely at the screen. "Yes," she said, feeling a flush of excitement. "That's us."

Cody advanced the film a little farther. "The drone was moving away, and I turned it to look down at the ground, trying to show what the people in the balloons were seeing. I'd done it earlier, but it was lighter outside. After taking this, I decided to stop filming that kind of footage because it was too dark to see anything. But I caught this just before I turned the drone back to the balloons."

"I can't make it out," Alex said.

"I can," Mary replied. "Those are the cars Martha saw. This must be when the kidnapping occurred." She peered closely. "But I can't see it very well. Just the headlights of the cars." She sighed with disappointment. "This isn't going to help us. I was hoping to see the vehicles clearly. Maybe the man who took her. Or even get a license plate number."

"You give up too easily," Cody said, grinning. Somehow, he zoomed in on the film until it was so fuzzy Mary couldn't make anything out. Then he did something else, and the picture grew sharper.

"I still don't see anything that tells us who this might be," Mary said, looking at Cody.

He pointed at the screen. "Right here. Which car is this, on the left?" he asked.

"I don't know," Mary said. "I'll have to ask Martha which car Da—the woman—was shoved into." Mary almost said the name Darlene but stopped herself at the last moment. Like Martha, she was about as sure as she could be that they were looking for Darlene, but she'd decided to keep that information to herself. Maybe after they talked to Darlene's father, they would have something besides pure speculation.

"Don't you see it?" Cody asked, pointing at a certain spot on the film.

Mary sighed and shook her head. "I just don't know what you—" It was then she saw...something. But what was it?

Cody reached into his bag and pulled out a photo. He pushed it toward Mary. "Here," he said. "Something is attached to the antenna. Now can you make it out?"

Mary nodded, her enthusiasm growing. "Yes, I see it. It looks like..."

"A deer," Alex said from behind her. Mary had almost forgotten he was there and was startled when he spoke. He leaned over her shoulder and picked up the photo. "Yes, I'm sure that's what it is. I've got a friend who's a hunter, and he has one, but it's the whole deer. This one is just the head."

Mary had seen antenna toppers before, but never a deer head. But that's exactly what it was.

"Will this help?" Cody asked.

"It's a clue," Mary said with a smile. "It should get us closer to the truth. The question is, does it belong to the kidnapper or his victim? Either way, we're further along than we were."

"I don't know," Alex said, putting the picture on the table and sitting down on the other side of Mary. "The police certainly can't question everyone who has a deer antenna topper."

"You're right," Mary said, "but if we find someone who could be our kidnapper and he has one on his car, it helps us persuade the police to check him out." She took a deep breath and let it out slowly. "Right now, we don't have anything solid. We have to keep going until we do."

"You're kinda like a detective, aren't you?" Cody asked.

Mary laughed. "No, not really. My sisters and I just don't like injustice. When we see something that isn't right..."

"You have to fix it?" Alex suggested. "I'm not sure you're a detective. You're more like a superhero."

Mary smiled at the thought of herself and her sisters wearing capes, endued with superpowers. "No," she said. "I think we're just too nosy for our own good."

Cody picked up the photo and handed it to her. "Well, superhero or detective, I hope this helps." He hesitated a moment. "Thanks for coming to my science fair," he said, his voice soft. "It...it was nice to have you there."

Mary smiled at him. "You're welcome. I really enjoyed it." She put the picture in her purse and stood up. She thanked Cody and Alex, who got up and offered to help her find her way out of the building. Mary was grateful. She was a little unsure where she was in relationship to the parking lot.

When they reached the right doors, Mary thanked Alex and took her umbrella out of her purse. He hesitated and stood with his hand on the door handle. Mary was surprised. She'd expected him to open it for her.

"Mary," he said, "I...I really enjoyed talking about old times." He gazed into her eyes. "It would be nice to get together...you know, to reminisce. Maybe over dinner sometime soon?"

Mary was taken aback by his invitation. Did he want to rekindle a friendship, or was it something more? She had no idea.

"Sure," she said. "We'll talk soon and plan something."

The corners of Alex's mouth twitched into a smile, and he held the door open. Mary stepped outside, opened her umbrella, and ran to her car. She could hardly wait to get home and tell her sisters about the new clue they had. They were one step closer to finding the woman they'd been looking for.

CHAPTER SEVENTEEN

So, Alex Wright asked you on a date?" Elizabeth asked Mary as she scooped some taco casserole out of the baking dish and onto her plate. They'd already prayed over their meal and were getting ready to eat.

Mary turned red. "I guess so," she admitted. She toyed with the edge of her napkin before finally settling it in her lap.

"Well, he seems like a nice guy," Elizabeth continued. "I guess it can't hurt to get to know someone a little better, can it?"

"I guess not," Mary agreed, but the hesitation in her voice made Martha wonder if she felt otherwise. Mary had seen a few men since her divorce from Brian, but nothing had really lasted, unless you counted her continued interest in Bill Richmond. Not that the future of Alex and Mary's possible relationship was the most important thing right now, anyway. Martha wanted her sister to be happy as much as Elizabeth did, but the whole point of Mary meeting up with Alex hadn't been to wrangle a dinner date. It had been to review the drone footage Cody had.

"So, you think the kidnapper had a deer topper on his car antenna?" Martha leaned forward in her chair and took a few quick bites of the casserole she'd heated up when she and Elizabeth had gotten back from the Feinsteins'. The casserole's colorful layers of corn, beans, salsa, jalapenos, chips, and cheese looked pleasing on the plate. The dish certainly wasn't the fanciest thing she'd ever made, but it sure was tasty and filling. A perfect comfort meal as they anticipated the onset of autumn.

"Actually, I don't know." Mary looked relieved to be changing the subject. "Cody was able to freeze the video and zoom in. We're positive that's what we saw, but which car belonged to the kidnapper, Martha? The one on the left or the right?"

Martha stared at her sister. "I think it was the one on the left. Or...no, it was the car on the right? Cheese and crackers...," she said in almost a whisper. Her mind felt frozen. Which car was the woman pushed into?

"You're not sure, are you?" Elizabeth asked.

Reluctantly, Martha shook her head. "I was so busy watching the woman I truly can't remember which car he put her in." She looked at her sisters, trying to blink back the tears that filled her eyes.

"Oh, Martha, it doesn't matter," Elizabeth said soothingly.

"Of course it does. How can we find the kidnapper if we don't know which car was his?"

"A clue is a clue," Mary said. "We won't give up looking for her. And besides, it could easily be the kidnapper's car."

"I guess," Martha said glumly.

"We're a step closer because of Cody's picture," Elizabeth said. "I refuse to view this in a negative light." She hesitated a moment. "You know, not too many people would have one of those on their car."

Martha thought about what Elizabeth said. "That's true, isn't it? I didn't even know such a thing existed. It probably means something to him. Or to Darlene." She put her fork down. "But which? Is he a hunter? Is Darlene an animal lover?"

"If it is his, I hope he didn't get rid of it," Elizabeth said.

Mary took a drink of iced tea and looked deep in thought. "I doubt he did," she finally said. "It was so dark that night, the kidnapper probably didn't see the drone flying overhead. He'd have no reason to think anyone saw any identifying details about his car."

Martha considered how she thought she'd seen the man look up at her after he pushed the woman into the car, but she didn't mention it.

"So, what do we do next?" she asked. "Drive around town until we find somebody with a deer head on their antenna? Then jump out and demand to know if they abducted someone?"

"Well, the first thing we do is ask Wanda if Darlene had one on her car," Elizabeth said. "We may have to ask Kathy's family the same thing."

"And in the meantime, we need to keep our eyes open for a car with a deer on the antenna," Martha said. "Just in case."

The kitchen was suddenly illuminated. Mary got up from her chair and looked outside. "It's John," she said. "Maybe he has news for us."

"Well, I hope it helps us eliminate someone," Martha said. "Two possible victims is giving me a headache."

"Oh, Martha," Elizabeth said, shaking her head.

Mary opened the door before John had time to knock. He came into the kitchen and sniffed the air. "Am I interrupting supper? Smells good."

Elizabeth laughed. "Taco casserole. Would you like some?"

John's grin made it clear he was interested. "If you insist," he said.

Elizabeth stood up and gestured toward an empty chair. "How about this? We'll trade you food for information."

John sat down. "I definitely have information, but I don't think you're going to like it."

Martha frowned at him. "What do you mean?"

"Kathy Gimble isn't your abductee."

"You found her?" Elizabeth asked.

"Well, she was found." He paused while Elizabeth put a plate of casserole in front of him.

"Is…is she okay?" Mary asked in a low voice.

"She will be," he answered. "I was told she was mugged before she left Lancaster. Had her car stolen. The perp hit her pretty hard and also grabbed her purse. Kathy was unconscious for quite some time. The hospital had no way to identify her. No car. No ID. She just woke up a few hours ago, and the hospital contacted her family."

"You said she'd recover?" Elizabeth asked.

"Yes, her prognosis is very good. She's lucky. Head injuries can be very serious."

Martha immediately thought of the woman she saw Friday night. What if she was badly injured…or worse? She pushed the frightening thoughts away so she could focus on John. "So she couldn't be our missing woman. She wasn't attacked at the festival."

"That's correct."

"Then it's Darlene," Mary said, her eyes wide. "We were right."

"Darlene who?" John asked.

While he ate, Elizabeth filled him in on their conversation with Wanda. When she was finished, John stood. "I'll need more than that to get officially involved," he said. "But keep me updated. And let me know what you find out from Darlene's father. He could file a missing person report for Darlene, you know."

"I'm sure he'd be happy to do that," Mary said. "What father wouldn't want the police to do everything they could to help find his missing child?"

"Let's not get ahead of ourselves," Elizabeth said. "We're still not one hundred percent sure Darlene is the person we're looking for."

Martha started to argue with her but thought better of it. Her sisters were doing everything they could to help find the woman.

"I checked with all the nearby hospitals just to see if they had anyone else come in for assistance with a head injury," John said, "but I couldn't find anything helpful."

"I thought you couldn't get involved until we had solid evidence," Elizabeth said with a smile.

John shrugged. "I didn't do much, but I thought it was important to make sure your abducted woman wasn't lying in a hospital bed somewhere."

"You're worried about her too, aren't you?" Martha asked.

He sighed. "I have to admit that I'm concerned. The more we find out, the more it seems someone's in trouble and needs help."

"It's Darlene," Mary said. "I agree with Martha."

"It's beginning to look that way," he said.

"You might be right," Elizabeth said.

"I thought you didn't want us to get ahead of ourselves," Martha said, trying not to sound too terse.

Elizabeth shrugged. "She's all we have, so I guess we have to keep going. We still have to follow up on the other suspects Wanda mentioned."

Martha got up and grabbed her notebook. She opened it and consulted her list. "The lawyer, D. Carlton, and the other customer."

"Yes," Elizabeth said. "We need to contact the lawyer. I'm not sure what to say. If we could just see his car, then we'd know if we're getting close. And we still have to figure out who the other customer is."

"And if we don't?" Martha asked. She hated to think what would happen if they couldn't press forward. The clock was ticking, and the more time that passed, the greater the chance the woman wasn't going to be recovered safely. If only Martha could remember which car was the kidnapper's.

Elizabeth sighed. "We can't give up now."

John looked at his watch. "I've got to get going," he said. "If I hear anything that might help you ladies, I'll let you know. I hope you'll do the same for me."

After they assured him they'd keep in touch, John left.

"What about the Feinsteins?" Mary finished her meal and carried her plate to the sink to rinse it off.

"I think we have a dead end there," Elizabeth said. "The woman Wanda thought Dan was having an affair with turned out to be his wife's long-lost biological mother."

"I didn't realize Gayla was adopted," Mary said.

"I guess it's not something that comes up that often in ordinary small talk," Elizabeth said. "Gayla's mom seems to be fitting nicely into the Feinsteins' life, though. And Dan and Gayla act as if they couldn't be happier."

"But what about the note Wanda saw Dan hand to Darlene?"

"Seems it was some information about their apple cider. They're hoping Hal will order some for the diner."

"So, all's well that ends well?" Mary asked with a smile.

"It looks that way."

Mary stifled a yawn and stood up from her seat. "I'm heading to bed. Today wiped me out."

"I need to get to sleep too," Elizabeth said, rising to her feet and depositing her dirty dishes in the sink. "I'm helping Rachel with her variety stand tomorrow morning."

Martha scooted her chair back from the table. "When are we going to visit the suspects on our list?"

"I probably need to work at the store in the afternoon, since I'll be gone all morning," Elizabeth said. "Maybe you can leave at one, when I get back from helping Rachel. Mary and I should be able to hold down the fort for the afternoon."

Martha agreed reluctantly. A few hours in the afternoon was better than nothing. She was trying not to worry, but she felt they were still missing important pieces of the puzzle. She could only pray that Darlene was safe.

CHAPTER EIGHTEEN

Bright and early Wednesday morning, Elizabeth got ready and drove to Rachel's variety stand on the side of Highway 340. It wasn't as busy as the main highway, but there was a steady flow of customers. The mornings were pleasantly cool now, and working outdoors, especially in the temperate autumn weather, brought its own delights. She loved running Secondhand Blessings with her sisters, but a change of pace every now and then never hurt anyone. How many times had their mother told them variety was the spice of life? Another perk of helping Rachel. Elizabeth had refused pay for her efforts, but Rachel always made sure to send her home with fresh produce or some kind of delicious baked good.

Talking with Rachel and spending time with her dear friend sweetened the deal too. "Good morning," Elizabeth called as she climbed out of her vehicle and walked toward Rachel. Rachel had already set up part of the day's wares on a long, folding table. Berry cobblers, apple crumble, and home-made whoopie pies, all tidily wrapped to keep flies and other pests out, were arranged neatly on the surface. Rachel also set out several baskets of fresh apples and assorted jars of jams, jellies, and preserves.

"*Guten morgen*," Rachel responded with a warm smile. "How do you fare this morning, Elizabeth?"

"Just fine," Elizabeth responded. She didn't mention the mystery of the missing woman to Rachel. She had told Martha the truth—she was invested in finding her. But Martha's efforts to locate Darlene, or whoever was missing, had been all-consuming. Elizabeth could do with a small break from mystery-solving, if only to let her mind rest.

Elizabeth chatted with Rachel for a few minutes as they finished setting up the table with items to sell. Before long, they started receiving a steady stream of customers. The whoopie pies went in a wink, and the apples sold quickly too. When they finally had a break in the activity, Elizabeth started to tell Rachel about their efforts to search for the woman Martha saw being abducted. A deep voice from behind her caused her to jump. She turned to see a straggly-looking man wearing a knit cap approach the table.

"How much are the pies?" he asked. "I don't see a tag."

The price Rachel quoted was modest, but the man just grumbled unintelligibly and started to shuffle back to his car, a rust-scored Pontiac.

"Wait, please," Rachel called after him. She carefully lifted a pie from the table and handed it to the man. "Would you consider this a gift?"

The man accepted the pie hesitantly. He looked as though he was suspicious of Rachel's kind offer, though he needn't be. Rachel was everything she presented herself to be—generous, kind, and thoughtful. Elizabeth was proud to be her friend.

"Do you accept exchanges?" The man set the pie down on a nearby stump and started to remove the watch from his wrist.

"Excuse me?" Rachel looked startled.

Elizabeth took charge of the situation. "We don't barter here. I'm sorry."

"Oh." The man fastened the watch back on his wrist. "Do you know any place that does?"

Elizabeth couldn't help but feel sorry for him. His clothes were worn and tattered, and from the looks of it, it was a wonder his car ran at all. Frankly, it didn't look as though he could afford even a few inexpensive jars of jam. She took a cue from Rachel's generous example. "I run a shop, Secondhand Blessings, with my sisters. Have you heard of it?"

The man shook his head.

"We accept gently used items on consignment." She gave him directions to the store.

"Thank you," the man finally mumbled before getting in his car.

As he pulled back onto the road, a familiar-looking vehicle drove up. Elizabeth was pleased to see it was John. He cast a glance over his shoulder at the retreating vehicle kicking up dust on the gravel road. Then he got out of his car and walked over to where Elizabeth and Rachel waited.

"That fellow's a bad apple," he said as he approached. "What was he doing here?"

It wasn't like John to dislike people. Elizabeth wondered what he meant. She felt a flicker of uneasiness in her stomach. "A bad apple?"

John heaved a sigh. "He's been in and out of the station so many times over the past year, I can't even count them. Passing bad checks, driving without a license, illegal gambling. He's bad news. Is this the first time he's come around here?"

"It is," Rachel said. A worried look creased her smooth features.

"I haven't seen him before," Elizabeth agreed.

"Just keep an eye out for him, then. I don't like him hanging around. Trouble has a way of following him. I don't want him causing you ladies any problems."

Elizabeth was touched by his concern, and she wondered if she'd made the right decision to invite the man to Secondhand Blessings. If he was in trouble with the law, was he a safe person to be around?

John climbed back into his patrol car and left. Elizabeth watched Rachel as she rearranged the wares on the table. Her friend seemed calm again, nonplussed that they'd been entertaining a criminal. "You were generous to give that pie away. What kind was it? I didn't recognize it."

"We call it 'Tears on My Pillow' pie." Rachel smiled. "I think it originally got its name because it can be difficult to bake. But it is also a good food to soothe a weary soul, which that man suffered from."

"You heard what John said about him. Doesn't that make you nervous? That he might be in trouble with the law? What if he comes back again now that you've given him a handout?"

Rachel's gaze was clear and warm as she studied Elizabeth. "People who are well have no need of a doctor, *ja?*"

Elizabeth nodded slowly, touched by Rachel's gracious response. She checked her watch. It was time to leave. She said goodbye to Rachel and got into her car. She kept thinking about Kathy Gimble. What if John was wrong about where she was attacked? He'd made it clear it was secondhand information. He wasn't directly connected to the case. It was a loose thread that she wanted to tie up herself so she could be certain. Besides, she also wanted to make sure Kathy was all right. Although she hadn't known her as well as her sisters, she had met her more than once when they were all younger.

She called the shop and told Mary she'd be a little late, then she headed to Lancaster General Hospital. She parked and went inside, stopping at the information desk to get Kathy's room number.

After getting the room number, she got onto the elevator. When she reached Kathy's floor, she stepped out but stopped in the hallway, feeling a little nervous and second-guessing herself. What if Kathy's family thought Elizabeth was a suspicious character? She turned back toward the elevators and was ready to punch the button for the ground floor when a woman called her name. Elizabeth turned back around and found one of the shop's customers standing on the other side of the hall, next to a room.

"Elizabeth, is that you?"

"Hello, Marybelle," Elizabeth said. "What are you doing here?"

"Unfortunately, I'm here to see my niece, Kathy. She was assaulted Friday night." Marybelle frowned. "Are you here to see her?"

Not knowing what else to do, Elizabeth nodded.

"Wow, you really care about your customers." Marybelle had a look of wonder on her face. "How did you know I was here?"

Feeling guilty, Elizabeth said, "I didn't. I knew Kathy when we were younger, and I heard about what happened. I just wanted to make sure she was okay."

Marybelle grabbed her arm and led her into the hospital room. "I'm sure she'll be happy to see you."

In the bed was a woman who resembled Marybelle. Another woman sat in a chair next to the hospital bed. Elizabeth assumed it was Kathy's mother. All three women shared a distinct Roman-shaped nose, red hair, and freckles. They were clearly related.

"Mimi, this is Elizabeth Classen from that shop I tell you about all the time. Secondhand Blessings?"

The woman in the chair looked a little surprised but covered it with a smile. "Are you in the hospital visiting someone?" she asked.

"No, I heard about Kathy's accident and wanted to see how she was doing," Elizabeth said. "She went to school with my sisters and me. It's been a long time, but I was concerned about her. We all are."

Although she hesitated a moment, Mimi said, "Kathy has so many friends. Thank you for coming by."

Elizabeth turned her attention to Kathy, who was watching her. Her scalp was covered with gauze.

"So how are you doing?" Elizabeth asked.

"Much better," Kathy said. Her voice was hoarse.

"She had a tube down her throat," Marybelle said, coming around and sitting on the other side of the bed. "It made her throat a little raw."

"I guess I was out until yesterday," Kathy continued. "My head still hurts, and I have a concussion, but it certainly could have been worse."

"I...I heard you were accosted in Lancaster?" Elizabeth asked.

"Where did you hear that?" Mimi's tone was sharp, and she had a frown on her face.

"Mom, quit giving Elizabeth the third degree," Kathy said. "I went to school with the Classen sisters." She looked at Elizabeth wistfully. "I'd love to see Mary and Martha too. Maybe when I get out, we could all have lunch."

"I think that's a lovely idea," Elizabeth said. "Do you have a release day yet?"

Kathy shook her head and grimaced. Obviously the movement had caused her pain. "Not yet, but I could call you when I'm home and ready for company."

"Please do." Elizabeth took a business card and a pen from her purse. She quickly wrote on the back of the card and handed it to Mimi. "The phone number of our store is on the front. My cell phone number is on the back. Please call us any time."

Kathy blinked back tears. "Thank you."

Mimi still looked suspicious of Elizabeth. "You never said where you heard about Kathy's accident."

Elizabeth tried to put the woman at ease. "I'm sorry. Officer John Marks is a friend of mine. He mentioned that Kathy had been injured."

Although she could have asked why a police officer in Bird-in-Hand who had nothing to do with the investigation knew details about her daughter, Elizabeth's explanation appeared to satisfy Mimi. "Yes, she was at a gas station when it happened," she said.

Elizabeth turned to Kathy, who was taking a sip of water from a glass on her nightstand, with Marybelle's help. "Have they caught the man who hurt you?"

Kathy shook her head. "No."

Mimi spoke up. "They haven't found her car either. We called and canceled all her credit cards, but she sure would like to have her driver's license returned. Hopefully, the police will find them."

"I hope they do too," Elizabeth said. "I don't want to tire you any more than I have, so I'll go. My sisters and I will be praying for you."

"Thank you," Kathy said and then leaned back into her pillow, looking tired.

After saying goodbye, Elizabeth slipped out of the room. She hurried to the elevator and got on when the doors opened. She'd planned on asking Kathy if she'd misplaced a charm from Girl Scout camp, but there wasn't any reason for it now, and Elizabeth didn't want Kathy or her mother to find the question odd. Although at first she'd felt uncomfortable about showing up at the hospital, at least now they knew for certain Kathy wasn't the person they were looking for. Even more importantly, Elizabeth had met someone who needed a friend.

CHAPTER NINETEEN

Martha looked up Darlene's father's telephone number and called him when she had a break at the shop. She was relieved when he answered. She wanted to talk to him as soon as possible, but she didn't want to upset him in case he wasn't aware that Darlene was missing. That kind of information was better said face-to-face. Although he acted a little confused as to why she wanted to stop by, he agreed to speak with her.

The morning seemed to crawl by. Would he be helpful? she wondered. Would he tell her that Darlene was in fact visiting her sister? If that was what Martha discovered, they were back to square one. Thankfully, Darlene would be safe, but some other woman could be in desperate trouble, and they'd have no idea who was missing. Doubts flew at Martha like wild birds. Had she created a false scenario? Maybe the woman she saw was already free. But if so, why wouldn't she have contacted the police? Or gone to the hospital for treatment? Thoughts churned round and round in her mind until it was almost one o'clock.

She kept checking the entrance, waiting for Elizabeth to return. She'd called to say she'd be a little late getting back. She wanted to stop by the hospital and check on Kathy. Finally, the doors opened, and Elizabeth stepped inside. The look on her face got Martha's attention, and she forgot about Darlene for a moment.

She walked up to the front of the shop and lowered her voice since Mary was talking to a customer a few yards away.

"Are you okay?" she asked Elizabeth. "Is Kathy all right?"

"She's recovering from a concussion, but she's going to be fine. She's not our victim. Kathy really was attacked in Lancaster. At a gas station." Elizabeth's eyes darted toward the older woman Mary was with. "There's something else," she whispered. "I may have made a mistake."

"What kind of mistake?"

Elizabeth took off her sweater and hung it up. "A man came by the variety stand. He didn't have much money. He looked… well, down on his luck. Rachel gave him some food, and then he asked her if he could barter for more." Elizabeth sighed.

"So you told him to come here." Martha wasn't asking a question. She knew Elizabeth's heart. "What's wrong with that?"

"John pulled up as the man was leaving. He told me the man was in and out of trouble all the time. He called him a 'bad apple.'"

Martha frowned. "That doesn't mean we can't work with him. We've had a few shady characters in here before. Everyone deserves a second chance."

"I know. I just hope I haven't caused us any trouble." Elizabeth looked at her watch. "You better get going. Are you still planning to talk to Darlene's father?"

"I called him, and he's agreed to see me."

Elizabeth must have heard the uneasiness in Martha's voice. She studied her closely. "You sound worried. Did he say something that bothered you?"

"No, it's not that," Martha said. "If he tells me that Darlene really is visiting her sister…"

"Then we have no idea who you saw being abducted Friday night."

"Exactly." Martha exhaled slowly. "Then what do we do?"

Elizabeth took Martha's hand. "We keep looking until we find that woman. What does your gut tell you, Martha?"

Martha considered Elizabeth's question seriously. Finally, she said, "I believe the missing woman is Darlene. I don't see how it could be anyone else."

"Good. Then go talk to…what was his name?"

"Clyde, I think? Yes, Clyde O'Neal."

"Go talk to him," Elizabeth said. "Whatever he tells us will help, I'm sure."

"I hope so," Martha said with a sigh. "I feel like I'm letting that poor woman down."

Elizabeth gave her a quick hug. "If I was ever abducted, I'd want you looking for me. You don't give up. I know you'd find me."

"Please don't get kidnapped," Martha said. "I don't think I could go through this again."

Elizabeth laughed. "Okay. I promise not to get kidnapped. Now get going."

Elizabeth went over to see if Mary needed any help, while Martha headed out the front doors.

It didn't take her long to get to Clyde's house. It was a small white clapboard house that could use a coat of paint, but the yard and the porch were neat and well kept. She went up to the front door and rang the doorbell. A few seconds later, the door swung open. An older man in a wheelchair was behind the storm door.

"You that lady that wants to talk to me about Darlene?" he asked.

"Yes, sir. I promise not to take up too much of your time." She grabbed the door he held open and waited while he backed up his wheelchair.

"Come on in," Clyde said. "Would you like a cup of coffee?"

"No, thank you."

Martha walked into a neat, orderly living room. It was obvious Clyde took pride in his home even if it was modest. Obviously, the outside paint job was too much for him. She made a mental note to check with a man at their church who had a home restoration company. He'd helped several elderly and ill people in their community. Maybe he could do something for Clyde.

Clyde gestured toward an overstuffed chair that matched his couch. She stroked the rich burgundy material. "I really like this," she said. "The color and texture are so appealing."

"I did that myself," he said with a touch of pride.

"You did?" Martha asked. "It's so professional looking."

"I had a small shop in town until…" He looked down at his wheelchair. "Until my accident. Now I do upholstery here in my house. People have to bring the furniture and the material. And pick the piece up when I'm done." He shrugged. "Of course, I don't make as much this way, but it's the only thing left for me."

"I'm sorry," Martha said, sitting down on the plush material. She couldn't help but think about some of her mother's furniture. It could use some refurbishing. "Do you mind if I ask about your accident?"

Clyde ran a hand through his wavy gray hair. His green eyes held a glint of sadness. "Tried to fix my roof myself. Fell and fractured my back." He slapped the sides of the wheelchair. "So now I wheel around instead of walking." He squared his shoulders. "I don't dwell on it. Doesn't help anything." He pointed his finger at Martha. "Now, let's get to Darlene. Is something wrong? After you phoned, I tried calling her, but her phone went straight to voice mail. She usually always calls me back right away, but I haven't heard from her."

Martha swallowed hard. What could she say that wouldn't worry Clyde? Besides being in a wheelchair, the man didn't look healthy. The pallor of his skin made it clear he was dealing with more than paralysis. She thought for a moment. "I just need to talk to her, Clyde," she said slowly. "Does she have any friends or family who might know where she is?"

Clyde shook his head. "She has a couple of friends, but she works so hard she doesn't have much time to socialize."

"What about relatives?" she asked again.

"We don't have any relatives. Darlene, me, and her mother. That was our family. Her mother died ten years ago. We don't have any other living kinfolk."

Martha stood. "If you hear from Darlene, will you let me know? My sisters and I own a business called Secondhand Blessings. You can reach me there." She pulled a card from her purse and handed it to him. "If you're concerned about her, you could file a missing person report with the police."

Clyde shook his head. "Nah, I'm sure that's not necessary. Darlene's taken off before, you know. After her mother died, she had a hard time. When she got too blue, she'd get in her car and go away for a while. To be by herself and think. It's been a long time since she's done that, but I'm sure she's fine."

Martha couldn't push him. She was afraid of frightening him. "It's probably something like that." She forced a smile. "I'm sure she'll show up."

Martha thanked Clyde and left. No sister. Darlene O'Neal was missing. Could she really have lied to get away for a while? Even as she considered the possibility, in her heart, Martha felt strongly that Darlene was the woman they were looking for.

Elizabeth was straightening out the table that held small kitchen appliances when the doors to the shop opened. The man she'd seen that morning at the variety stand walked in, his eyes darting around the shop. She took a deep breath and approached him.

"Hello again," she said. "What can I do for you?"

The man reached into the pocket of his tattered jacket and pulled out a watch. "I...I want to sell this. How much can you give me for it? You have to help me."

His voice rose, and his eyes grew wide. Elizabeth didn't like the way he made her feel. Mary left the customer she was with and came up next to them.

"Is anything wrong?" she asked Elizabeth.

Before she could answer, the doors opened, and John walked in. He immediately approached the man. "Time to go, Arnold," he said. "You need to leave these ladies alone."

"I can be here if I want to," he insisted.

John looked at Elizabeth. "Is he causing any trouble?"

Elizabeth shook her head. "John, can I talk to you a moment?" She gestured to a spot a few feet away.

"You have every right to ask him to leave," John said as he joined her. "If he's causing a problem…"

"That's not it," Elizabeth whispered. "Wanda told us that Darlene dated a guy for a while. I'm sure she said his name was Arnold. Could this be him? Could he be involved in her disappearance?"

"I don't know, but to be honest, I don't believe he could pull off something like that. I think he lives in his car."

"Then it probably isn't the right Arnold," Elizabeth said, disappointed.

John shrugged. "I have no idea. He used to have a job and a place to live, so it's not impossible. But he's really gone downhill over the past year or so. We think he's involved in something he shouldn't be. We suspect there's an illegal gambling ring in the area, but so far we haven't been able to find it." He looked over at Arnold and frowned.

"I'm goin', I'm goin'," Arnold said. He glared at Elizabeth. "Nice way to treat customers."

Although she wanted to help the man, it was clear that John didn't think it was a good idea. She didn't respond to the man's challenge, just stayed silent.

The man gave all three of them a nasty look and left.

"I feel sorry for him," Mary said.

"He really is bad news," John said. "I was driving by and happened to see his car pulling in here. I'm glad I stopped. Frankly, I'm sorry he got a look inside the shop. Make sure everything is locked up tight for the next few nights and that your alarm is on."

"You really think he might try to break in?" Mary asked.

"Yes. I believe he's behind a lot of thefts in our area. We just haven't been able to catch him with the goods."

"I'm still concerned that he might have something to do with Darlene's disappearance," Elizabeth said. "Wanda told us Darlene's ex-boyfriend Arnold keeps hanging around the diner."

John shrugged. "I guess we can't rule it out, but like I said, he just doesn't strike me as someone who's capable of kidnapping someone. We've never had anyone accuse him of being physically aggressive. He's just a thief."

At that moment, the door opened again, and Martha came in, her eyes wide. "That man," she said, gesturing toward the parking lot. "Who is he?"

Elizabeth told her what had just occurred.

"That's the man I saw outside the Two Bird Monday night," Martha said. "After I talked to Wanda."

Elizabeth gasped. "Are you sure?"

"His knit hat gives it away. Such an ugly green color. I'm sure it's the same person."

Had Elizabeth's offer to help the man just narrowed their search?

CHAPTER TWENTY

Elizabeth gestured toward the door where Arnold had exited. "That's the same man I saw at the variety stand this morning. Remember, I told you about how I stuck my foot in my mouth and invited him to the store?" Elizabeth felt foolish. She'd been so eager to follow Rachel's shining example that she'd been reckless in the process. What if the man really was a dangerous criminal? What if his poor, downtrodden demeanor had been an act, designed to appeal to their pity?

"You're too hard on yourself." John shook his head at Elizabeth. It was as though he was reading her mind. "You don't need to apologize for being kind. It's one of the things I admire about you." His earnest, intense gaze filled her stomach with butterflies, a feeling she was growing accustomed to when he was around.

"It wouldn't hurt her to be more cautious, though," Martha said. "If John is suspicious of the guy, I consider that a pretty good litmus test. What did you say his name was again?"

"Arnold," John said. "Arnold Kopeckni."

"We need to check with Wanda and see if he's the guy she was talking about, although I doubt there are a lot of Arnolds running around in Bird-in-Hand."

Elizabeth shook off her flustered emotions and turned toward Martha. "You seem pretty confident that Darlene's the person we're looking for. I take it she's not visiting her sister?"

"Definitely not visiting her sister." Martha looked at John. "Her sister doesn't exist. Clyde said Darlene is an only child. Doesn't have any family to speak of outside of him, really."

Elizabeth frowned. "So either Darlene was lying or…"

"What?" Martha asked.

"Someone really did force her to make that phone call."

"I think that's entirely possible," Martha agreed.

John went to the doorway, looking in the direction Arnold had disappeared. Elizabeth wondered if he was monitoring the woods around their house for evidence of Arnold's return. What if Arnold really had abducted Darlene? The thought gave her the shivers.

"John?"

"Hmm?" John turned from the entrance but still looked distracted.

"Did you come by the store for anything in particular? Is there any information about a missing person?"

John turned to face her. "No, unfortunately, there's no new info. I actually stopped by to see if you were free for dinner tonight. I'm thinking a steak from the Stockyard sounds pretty good."

Elizabeth remembered the earnest gaze he'd given her a few minutes earlier, and her worried thoughts fled from her mind. Her heart raced. "I think I'm free." She looked at her sisters for confirmation, and they nodded.

"You deserve a night off," Mary said. "You've been pulling double duty, working the variety stand and the store. Go have fun."

"I want to see if I can talk to Wanda tonight," Martha said. "By the way, does any of our furniture need to be reupholstered?"

Elizabeth tilted her head to one side. What was Martha talking about? "Reupholstered? We just redecorated our own rooms not too long ago. Are you planning on tackling the rest of the house?"

"Not exactly," Martha said. "It's a long story, but Darlene's father owns an upholstery business from his house. He's a little down on his luck, but he's still trying to take in as much work as he can. I'd like to help him."

Elizabeth smiled. For all her outward prickles, Martha did have a gentle heart under her tough exterior. Elizabeth knew they'd be missing some pieces of furniture in the near future.

Elizabeth walked through the front door of the Stockyard Inn and breathed deeply. The mouth-watering aroma of grilled seafood and steak filled the air. The last time she'd been here with John, many months before, they'd left in a hurry, hot on the trail of an antiques thief. Would she return home tonight to find that Arnold had broken into Secondhand Blessings? The man had seemed so desperate to sell his watch. It looked old, like a family heirloom. Was he really bad news, like John said? Or was he just having a rough time? Jesus had instructed His followers to care for the poor. Shouldn't she give Arnold the benefit of the doubt? John certainly didn't think so.

"Mmm, I'm hungry," she said, turning her attention toward John.

"I am too." He smiled. "I'm glad they're not too busy yet. We should get seated soon."

At his words, a slim hostess clad in black approached them. "If you'd follow me, please, I'll show you to your table."

John stepped aside to let Elizabeth take the lead. She felt a tiny edge of self-consciousness as she walked ahead of John, but it wasn't an entirely unpleasant feeling. She'd dressed up a little more than usual tonight, even putting on a bit of lipstick and borrowing a beaded bag of Mary's.

The hostess led them to their table, and John pulled out Elizabeth's chair for her. "You look lovely tonight," he said as he took his own chair.

"Thank you." She felt flattered by his attention, as she always did, but something was slowly changing. In the time she'd known him, she'd always kept her feelings on hold when it came to John. He didn't share her faith, the most important thing in her life. The defining component that made her who she was. Yet he'd shown signs of softening his attitude lately. He'd attended church on his own before, though he said he wasn't interested in attending regularly. At least, not yet.

Looking at him standing beside her, so relaxed and happy, Elizabeth couldn't help but let the words she was thinking spill out, openly and honestly. "I enjoy spending time with you, John."

John smiled down at her. "I feel the same about you. That's why I suggested we go out for dinner tonight."

Elizabeth didn't want to risk ruining the moment they shared, but she felt the timing was right. After all, if she and John were going to be a good match at some point in the future, they had to agree on the most important things or their relationship wouldn't work anyway. "You haven't visited Mount Zion in a while. Would you be interested in coming to church with me this Sunday?"

She was relieved to see that he didn't seem uncomfortable.

"I might. I'm not working that day," he said slowly. "Can I let you know a little later in the week?"

"Of course." Elizabeth was delighted that John was open to her offer, but she didn't want to push it any further and spook him. She opened her menu and studied the meal options. John decided on the steak he wanted in about two seconds and set the menu aside to look around the restaurant.

A moment later, he gestured toward a man sitting at a table tucked into a corner on the other side of the room. "Do you know who that is?"

Elizabeth glanced over her shoulder at a slightly familiar-looking man hunched over a file folder of paperwork spread out on the table before him. "Refresh my memory?"

"Denver Carlton." She must have looked blank because he continued. "He's the prosecuting attorney for Lancaster. We cross paths quite a bit, given the nature of our work."

A light bulb went off in her brain. Denver Carlton? D. Carlton? He had to be the lawyer Wanda said was at the Two Bird the night Darlene went missing. She realized she'd seen his face before. On the local news broadcasts. A drawn-out trial had been going on for the last few weeks, and his picture had been splashed across the screen quite a bit.

She searched her memory. What had Wanda said about him? That he'd been meeting with a woman who'd acted nervous. She replayed Wanda's words in her mind. *Jumpier than a jackrabbit. Every time I set the coffeepot down, she startled.*

"Maybe I should talk to him," John said. "See if he knows anything about your missing woman. You did say that waitress at the Two Bird mentioned that he was acting suspicious, right?"

Elizabeth nodded, her throat tight.

John continued. "If he gives me a straight answer, we'll be one step ahead."

"And if he doesn't?"

John looked grim. "Well, then we can probably assume he's hiding something. And that's a step forward in its own right."

CHAPTER TWENTY-ONE

"Guten morgen, Martha." Rachel's voice rang out as clear and crisp as the beautiful day she ushered in through the doors of Secondhand Blessings. "May I set up in our usual place?"

How had Martha forgotten that Rachel's quilting circle was meeting at the store today? She'd hoped the morning would be quiet so she could sneak into the storeroom and make a few phone calls to gather more information about Darlene.

"I'm so sorry, Rachel." Martha slapped a hand to her forehead. "If I look surprised, it's because I am. It slipped my mind that today was Thursday."

Rachel smiled. "You look as though you are carrying the weight of the world on you. There is much on your mind?"

Not necessarily much on her mind, but rather one thing. How to find Darlene before something awful happened. It was all Martha could focus on lately. It had been almost a week. Were they too late to help her? If she'd been kidnapped for money, where was the ransom note? She sighed. "I suppose I am worrying."

Rachel set her bags on the counter. "My *maam* always used to say 'sufficient unto the day is the evil thereof.'"

"Your mother was a wise woman," Martha said. It was true she shouldn't worry about what might happen. Borrowing trouble certainly never helped anyone, but worry was a tough habit to break.

Martha cleared some items out of the way and helped Rachel set up a circle of chairs for the quilting ladies, just as Elizabeth rushed into the store. Martha hadn't had a chance to speak with Elizabeth since her dinner date with John. She'd been in bed by the time Elizabeth arrived home, and this morning, Elizabeth had still been getting ready when Martha left to open up the store.

Elizabeth stopped in front of Martha. "You won't believe what I found out."

"What?" From Elizabeth's excited tone, Martha knew it had to be something interesting. She wasn't expecting the next words out of Elizabeth's mouth though.

"I think I know who our kidnapper is."

Martha's mind spun. Who could it possibly be? How could Elizabeth be so confident she knew the truth? She started to ask Elizabeth to explain her comment, but her words were cut off as more ladies arrived for the quilting circle. One of them had some lovely handmade aprons to sell to the store, and Elizabeth hurried away to take care of the items at the counter. Martha exchanged pleasantries with the ladies as they settled in to sew, though it took every ounce of patience she had.

Martha waited until Elizabeth finished up at the front. "So who is the kidnapper?" she asked quietly.

"You're never going to believe it," Elizabeth whispered. "I was at dinner with John last night, and just as we sat down to order, he saw someone he knew across the room."

"Who?"

A few ladies from the quilting circle glanced up from their projects, and Martha realized her voice had risen far above Elizabeth's whisper. She smiled at the women, who exchanged confused looks, then refocused on the sewing work in their laps.

Elizabeth continued. "It's—" Her sentence was interrupted as an older Amish man and woman entered the store. Heinrich and Faith Schrock were longtime friends, and Faith was part of Rachel's quilting circle.

Martha clamped her teeth together to keep from revealing her frustration.

"Faith, I am so glad you could come." Rachel stood to welcome the woman who had just entered, then she turned to address the man. "Did you enjoy the balloon festival last week, Heinrich?"

Martha started to turn back to Elizabeth and finish their conversation, but Heinrich's next words caught her ear.

Heinrich grunted at Rachel's question. "We did not attend the festival, though I wish we had for all the trouble it caused."

Rachel frowned. "Trouble?"

Faith swatted her husband's arm. "Heinrich is just upset because the extra traffic caused some noise at our home."

Heinrich snorted. "Extra traffic? More like one car that drove back and forth on our road for hours. A fly in the ointment, he was. I am glad the festival is over. No more lurkers outside our house."

"We do not know that he had any bad intent, Heinrich," Faith said. "People are free to drive where they like on public property."

"That's odd," Elizabeth said, jumping into the conversation. "Why would someone spend that much time on your road?"

"Heinrich exaggerates," Faith said. "The man was not there for hours. It was still light when we first noticed him, and right before dusk when he left."

"He didn't leave right away though." Heinrich's eyebrows furrowed. "When I went out to take care of the animals, I took a flashlight and walked down the road."

"Heinrich!" Faith gasped. "You were spying?"

"I was not." Heinrich looked indignant. "I was watching over my home. And I am glad I was. The man acted suspicious. He parked in that old store lot, with his headlights on."

An old store lot? Martha's heart began to pound. "Where does your family live?"

"Our farm is just off the highway," Faith replied. "Across the street from Greer's Hardware. It is closed down now though."

Greer's Hardware. The parking lot Darlene was abducted from. It was too uncanny to be a coincidence. Perhaps Heinrich had seen something that would prove useful. "Who was driving the car? Did you get a glimpse of him?"

Heinrich shook his head. "I could not see his face. There was something written on the side of his car, though. The name of a company, I believe."

"What name?"

Heinrich stroked his beard. "Let me think…. It was something that started with an *R*. Had a drawing on the side too."

"A drawing of what?" If Heinrich told the story any slower, Martha was sure she would boil over like a teapot on the stove.

"It was a key."

A key? What could that possibly mean? A locksmith?

Faith touched her husband's shoulder. "Heinrich, I planned to quilt today."

Heinrich didn't reply immediately, just grunted again. "I will leave you to it then." He bid goodbye to the ladies, who all went back to their sewing, leaving Martha and Elizabeth free to talk.

"What do you think of that?" Martha asked.

Elizabeth frowned. "I'm not sure. I'm rather certain the person Heinrich saw wasn't the kidnapper."

"What makes you think that?"

"Like I said, I believe I saw the kidnapper last night. John and I were having dinner, when John recognized someone. He looked familiar to me too, though I didn't place him at first."

"Who was it?" Martha took a breath. "And if one more person comes through that door, I will tell them kindly that they need to wait." She trained her eyes on the door, but this time, no one appeared to interrupt Elizabeth's declaration.

"I think it's the prosecuting attorney, Martha. Denver Carlton."

A vague memory floated to the surface of Martha's mind. She did watch the news on occasion and remembered seeing Denver's face associated with an ongoing case in Lancaster.

Elizabeth continued. "He was acting so suspicious. John tried to talk to him about the balloon festival and about Darlene's disappearance, but he clammed up. Wouldn't discuss anything with John. John even mentioned that Wanda had seen him at the Two Bird recently, and he denied he'd eaten there in the last year."

"Do you think Wanda's lying about seeing him there?"

"I don't know why she would. What motive would she have?"

Martha scratched her head. From where she was sitting, Carlton certainly looked suspicious. But then again, so did the person driving the key car near Heinrich and Faith's.

"None that I can think of," Martha replied. "So other than acting strangely, what makes you think that Denver Carlton is the kidnapper?"

"John and I were seated near the window of the restaurant, and we saw Carlton get in his car when he left."

"And?"

"He had a topper on his antenna, Martha. What are the chances?"

CHAPTER TWENTY-TWO

Mary was running late. After feeding the animals, she'd noticed one of the goats, Blynken, seemed a little lethargic, which wasn't his normal temperament. He was a friendly little thing who loved attention. Mary tried not to show it, but he was actually her favorite. She called Dr. Goodrich, the veterinarian who took care of the goats. He promised to come out and look at Blynken later in the afternoon. The little goat was eating, but he didn't attack his food the way he usually did. Mary sat down on the ground and cuddled with him a bit. According to Elizabeth, the other goats, Wynken and Nod, weren't as friendly as Blynken when they first came to live on the Classen farm, but they were changing and now allowed themselves to be petted from time to time. At the moment, however, their only interest was in their food.

After a few minutes, Mary hugged Blynken one more time and got to her feet. "Dr. Goodrich will be here to look at you a little later," she told him.

She went inside, washed her hands, and hurried to the shop. When she got there, Martha and Elizabeth had their heads together, talking. Mary said hello to the ladies in the quilting circle and went over to join them.

"Everything okay?" Martha asked, frowning.

Mary explained about Blynken and told her she'd called Dr. Goodrich.

"I'm sure he's fine," Elizabeth said. "Maybe he ate something that didn't agree with him."

"I suppose it's possible," Mary said. She shrugged. "I guess we'll have to wait until the doctor can take a look at him. I hate seeing him like that. He's such a sweet little thing." She looked back and forth between her sisters. "What were you talking about?"

"We may have a break in our search for Darlene," Martha said.

"What do you mean?"

Elizabeth told her about seeing Denver Carlton at the restaurant the night before. "John talked to him, and he denied eating at the Two Bird in the last year. Yet Wanda said she saw him there the night Darlene disappeared. He appeared to be really nervous about something."

"And when he went out to the parking lot, they saw his car," Martha said. "And guess what was on top of his antenna?"

Martha's smug expression made Mary's guess easy. "A deer antenna topper?"

"Exactly."

Mary noticed that Elizabeth didn't seem to share Martha's enthusiasm. "It was a deer topper, wasn't it, Elizabeth?" she asked.

Elizabeth grimaced. "Well, it was dark by the time he left the restaurant. I couldn't really tell exactly what the topper was." She shrugged. "But really, how many people do you know who even have those on their car?"

"So you're not sure that it was him?" Mary asked, frowning.

"I was sure last night. And this morning. But then Faith's husband, Heinrich, told us about a man driving up and down the road in front of their farm the night of the balloon festival. It certainly sounds suspicious."

"I don't understand," Mary said. "What does this have to do with anything?"

"He also saw him in the parking lot of Greer's Hardware, parked with his lights on," Martha said.

"Well, that does sound suspicious," Mary said. "Could that have been Denver Carlton?"

"Heinrich said there was writing on the side of the man's car," Elizabeth replied. "Denver Carlton drives a black BMW. Trust me, there's no writing on the side."

Martha sighed. "So this is someone else."

"Yes," Elizabeth said. "And then there's Arnold. John doesn't trust him, but he doesn't think he's capable of kidnapping anyone. Frankly, I'm a little confused."

Martha sighed with exasperation. "I called Wanda to confirm that the Arnold who showed up at the shop is the same Arnold that Darlene dated for a while. It's him. She described him to a T. Wanda said he started asking Darlene for money. She finally had to walk away from him. He didn't take it very well." She took a deep breath and let it out slowly. "I know what John said about him, but we've got to follow every lead. Darlene is missing and could be in more trouble than we realize. She's been gone almost a week now, and we still have no idea where she is."

"We're doing our best, Martha," Mary said. "I think we need to follow up on this Denver Carlton guy first. He sounds the most likely. He had the antenna topper on his car, and he lied."

"Who had an antenna topper?" a man asked from behind the women.

Mary jumped at the sound. She hadn't been paying attention to who had come into the shop and apparently, neither had her sisters. She turned and found Alex standing there.

"A man named Denver Carlton," she said after greeting him. "Do you know him?"

"I don't know him personally, but his daughter Eppie goes to my school. I'm not surprised about the topper though."

"What do you mean?" Martha asked.

"The glee club sold them for a fundraiser," Alex said. "There's probably quite a few of them around town."

Mary's mouth dropped open. "Why didn't you tell me that while we were looking at Cody's footage?"

Alex turned red. "I...I'm sorry. It slipped my mind. I got distracted."

"So Denver might not be our guy at all?" Elizabeth asked.

Alex looked confused. "What guy?"

"The guy who kidnapped the woman I told you about," Mary said.

"I remember. No, he's a straight arrow. Has a wife and three kids. Sings in his church choir. Again, I'm sorry. Hope I haven't made things harder for you."

Mary smiled. "You kept us from giving the name of an innocent man to the police."

The front door opened, and Martha went to greet a local woman who'd brought in several antiques that she had inquired about selling to the shop.

"Why did you stop by, Alex?" Mary asked. "Shouldn't you be at school?"

"I called in a substitute," he said. His expression turned serious. "I wanted to let you know that..."

"Let who know what?" Martha had rejoined them.

"That was fast," Elizabeth said.

Martha shrugged. "The check was already written. I just handed it to her. She was very happy with the amount."

Mary let out a long, exaggerated sigh. She looked at Alex. "Let me know what?"

"Cody didn't show up for school today," he said. "When the school called his parents, they had no idea where he was."

Mary swallowed hard. "Are you saying that Cody is missing?"

"I have no idea if he ran away, or if he just skipped school," Alex said. "I made an excuse to the principal and requested someone else to cover my class. I think Principal Belson knew why I wanted to leave and was happy to know I would search for Cody."

Mary shook her head. "Do you have any idea where he might be?"

Alex shrugged. "I honestly don't. I thought you might like to come with me. He really seemed to like you. If we can find him, maybe he'd talk to you. We could drive to some of the places where he usually hangs out. At this point I don't know what else to do."

"Didn't you say his parents don't pay much attention to him?" Elizabeth asked.

"They're not bad parents," Alex said slowly, "but they work so hard, they don't spend much time with him. I think he resents it. I'm afraid a lot of parents make the same mistake."

"Can you spare me for a while?" Mary asked her sisters. "I really would like to help look for Cody."

"Of course," Elizabeth said. "I'll pray God leads you to the right spot."

Martha put her hand on Mary's shoulder. "Cody is blessed to have someone like you in his life. Hopefully, you'll find him quickly and get him home."

"I'm not sure that will solve the problem though," Mary said. "Can you speak to his parents, Alex? Maybe you could get them to realize they need to make some changes."

"It's a fine line to maintain, since I'm his teacher. I have to be careful. It might be better to ask our school counselor to meet with all three of them."

Mary smiled. "That would be wonderful. Will you do it?"

"I think Cody disappearing from school might be just the catalyst for a meeting like that. I'll get to work on it. But first we need to find him."

Mary heard the doors open behind them and saw Elizabeth smile.

"I don't think that will be too tough," she said. "He just walked in."

CHAPTER TWENTY-THREE

Mary, Cody, and Alex sat at the kitchen table inside the house, waiting for Cody's parents. Alex had called them to let them know Cody was okay and that he was with them.

"I still don't understand why you didn't go to school," Mary said. "If you wanted to see me, you could have waited until after your classes."

Cody shrugged as he stared down at the table, refusing to meet her eyes. He hadn't said much since showing up on their doorstep.

She leaned in closer to him. "Talk to me, Cody. Please. I feel as if we're friends. If there's anything I can do to help you…"

He finally raised his face, tears washing his eyes. "I just wanted to be with someone who cares about me. And about what's important to me."

"Your parents care, Cody," Alex said. "They're just busy with their jobs. I'm sure they don't want you to feel badly."

"What triggered this?" Mary asked. "What was it about today that made you not want to go to school?"

Cody shook his head and didn't respond.

"I think I know," Alex said with a sigh. "Yesterday we displayed all the science projects in the high school gym. It was a chance for family and students who couldn't attend the science fair to see the projects. Cody's project was highlighted because he won."

"But no one showed up," Cody said. "No one. My mom promised to take off work and be there, but she texted me at the last minute and said she couldn't come." He wiped away a tear that snaked down his cheek. "I stood there by myself, like an idiot, while everyone else had family that took the time to be there."

"I'm sorry," Mary said. "I really am."

"I know you came to the science fair to talk to me about the drone footage. You didn't have to stay, but you did. You even waited around for them to pick the winner."

Mary smiled at him. "I'm glad I was there. I really am, but skipping school wasn't a good idea."

"She's right, Cody," Alex said. "When I talked to your parents, they were really worried."

He grunted. "They were probably just upset because they had to leave work."

"I wish I could convince you—" Alex stopped talking at the sound of a car outside.

Mary got up and looked out the window. A nice-looking couple got out of a car and walked up the porch steps. She went to the front door and opened it.

"Is Cody Stephens here?" the woman asked.

"Yes, he is." Mary held the door open, and the couple came in. Cody's mother was an attractive woman with dark hair like her son's. She was small and nicely dressed, but her face was tight with worry. His father wore a suit that looked expensive. Although he was a good-looking man, he had tired eyes.

"Cody, what in the world were you thinking?" he asked when he saw his son sitting at the table.

Cody didn't answer, just gazed down again.

"I asked you a question, young man," Mr. Stephens said a little more sharply.

"Nolan, don't be rude," his wife said, extending her hand to Mary. "I'm LeeAnn. Thank you so much for letting us know where to find him. We were so worried."

"I'm sorry," her husband said. "I'm Nolan."

Mary shook his hand as well.

"Thank you for calling us, Mr. Wright," Nolan said.

Mary gestured toward the kitchen table. "Please sit down. Can I get you something? Coffee? Tea?"

"No, thank you," Nolan said. "We just want to get our boy and take him back to school."

Ignoring her husband, LeeAnn sat down and smiled at Mary. "Actually, I'd love a cup of coffee. As long as it's not too much trouble."

"Not at all."

Nolan stood staring at his wife for a moment, but he finally sat down. "So what's going on, Cody?" he asked. "I think you owe us an explanation."

"Cody," LeeAnn said, reaching over and putting her hand on her son's arm, "please talk to us. We can't help if we don't understand."

Mary glanced at Alex. She felt like Cody wanted to tell them how he felt but didn't know how. Alex met her glance and nodded.

"If you don't mind," he said, "I think Cody finds it difficult to tell you what's bothering him. Do you mind if I poke my nose in?"

Although Nolan didn't say anything, his expression made it pretty clear he was irritated with his son's silence.

"Please," LeeAnn said. "We really want to understand."

Alex took a deep breath. "I know that you care about Cody. But I think he's feeling a little...overlooked lately."

"Overlooked?" Nolan's eyebrows shot up. "We do everything we can to support our son. We even bought him a drone and everything that goes with it so he can follow his passion. We give him a nice place to live, food, clothes...everything he needs."

LeeAnn sighed. "I think I know what this is all about, Nolan. I've told you more than once—"

"I'm not going to argue about this in front of strangers, LeeAnn." Nolan's brusque retort caused Cody to jump.

Mary turned to pour a cup of coffee and then came back to the table just in time to see Cody finally raise his head.

"Don't talk to her like that, Dad," he said. "It's not...nice."

Nolan's face fell. "I'm sorry, Son," he said. "You're right." He shook his head. "I'm sorry, honey. I get used to handing out orders at work and forget that I shouldn't talk to my family like that."

Mary was pretty sure his employees didn't like it much either, but she kept her opinion to herself.

"Is this because we missed your science fair?" Nolan asked, his tone more controlled.

"I think it's more than just the science fair," LeeAnn said. "We're not around enough, Nolan. A boy needs his parents to be involved in his life. We're always at work. Something's got to change."

"Kids really do need their parents as they're growing into adulthood," Alex interjected. "Their teenage years can be very confusing. Maybe it's not possible for you to cut back on your hours—I don't know your situation—but I do know Cody's a good kid and he could use your support. Your availability."

LeeAnn sighed. "I've been thinking about going part time. And Nolan, you could try harder to be home at night and on the weekends."

"I suppose," Nolan said, "but we won't make as much money. We'll have to cut back on some things."

"I don't care about that, Dad," Cody said, his voice shaking. "I just want time with you and Mom. I feel so alone."

"Oh, Cody." LeeAnn scooted her chair closer to his and wrapped her arms around her son. "I'm sorry, honey. We'll fix this."

Mary sat down at the table. "You know, my parents didn't make a lot of money, but this home was always full of love. My sisters and I thought it was the most wonderful place in the world. We still do. After all these years we ended up back here. We wouldn't trade it for the fanciest house in town." She hesitated. "I guess what I'm trying to say is that *things* didn't matter to us. Our best memories aren't about what we owned. They're all about the time we spent together."

LeeAnn picked up a napkin from the table and dabbed her wet cheeks. "I grew up on a farm," she said to Mary, smiling through her tears. "We weren't rich, but we were very happy. I want that for Cody." She looked at her husband. "I think we have some work to do."

"There's a great counselor at the school," Alex said. "I think she could really help you."

"I don't know if I want to share my personal life with someone I don't know," Nolan said slowly.

"Oh, Nolan," LeeAnn said, "we just did. And it's helped. We would love to meet with her." She smiled at Mary. "Thank you for putting up with us, but I think we need to go home and talk. Really talk. Besides, we shouldn't bother you any longer. You've been so kind."

Mary looked at the cup in front of LeeAnn. "You're welcome to stay and finish your coffee."

"Thank you. Maybe another time." LeeAnn stood. She narrowed her eyes at her husband. "Let's go, Nolan. We'll call the school and tell them Cody will be back tomorrow. We also need to call work and let them know we're taking the rest of the day off. Let's all go home." She put her hand on Cody's cheek. "It's been a long time since I made those fudge cookies you like so much. How about I bake a batch?"

Cody smiled for the first time since his parents had entered the house. "That sounds great, Mom." He put his arms around her in a big hug.

Nolan stayed seated, his head down. Mary could almost see him wrestling with himself. Finally, he said, "Seems I'm off work the rest of the day." He looked at Alex. "Can you give me the name of that counselor you mentioned?"

Alex reached into his pocket and took out his billfold. After searching through the contents, he pulled out a card. "Here you go," he said, handing it to Nolan.

Nolan took the card and put it in his coat pocket. Then he stood up. "Let's go," he said to his wife and son.

"Thank you for all your help," LeeAnn said to Mary and Alex. "We really appreciate it."

"Yes, we do." Nolan shook hands with both of them.

"Thank you," Cody said softly.

"You're welcome, Cody," Mary said, trying to keep her voice steady. She was grateful to be involved in seeing his family draw closer together.

Alex got up and walked them to the door, and then he closed it behind them. "Wow," he said. "That was intense." He smiled at Mary. "Maybe you should be a counselor. What you said about the way you were raised really helped."

Mary chuckled. "I wasn't sure I should say anything at all. I just get riled up sometimes and speak my mind. My sisters say it's a curse...and a blessing. I'm not sure that's such a good thing."

"I think it is," Alex said softly. "Mary, please have dinner with me tonight." His gaze bored into hers. "Not as friends. I'm asking you for a date."

Mary was caught off guard. "Okay," she said impulsively. "I'd like that."

"Great." Alex stood up and headed for the door. "I'm leaving before you change your mind. I'll pick you up at seven."

Mary second-guessed herself as he walked out the door and headed to his car. She'd been happy about the progress between Cody and his parents, but now she felt unsettled. Alex's invitation had come so quickly she hadn't had much time to think. Should she have agreed?

Suddenly, Bill's face drifted into her mind. If they were only friends, why couldn't she stop thinking about him?

CHAPTER TWENTY-FOUR

Martha waited anxiously for Dr. Goodrich to arrive. He was slated to arrive any minute, but she could only hope he showed up sooner rather than later. Mary had filled her in on Blynken's condition—no energy, little appetite—and had told Martha that the doctor hadn't seemed overly concerned. She wanted the vet to check in on the little guy and make sure he hadn't gotten ahold of something bad to eat. Their goats had chomped down many odd things over the years, but they had stomachs of steel and rarely got ill. That increased her concern.

Blynken's condition must have worsened since Mary last saw him though. He lay on his side in the straw, chewing methodically. Martha tried to peer in his mouth, but whenever she tried, he kept his teeth clamped shut. At least he was breathing okay. She thought about going back to the house to call Dr. Goodrich's office again and see if they could hurry things along, but she didn't want to leave the little goat. He was clearly in quite a bit of pain.

Thankfully, the vet showed up just about the time she was thinking of running to get her cell phone. He knelt down in the packed dirt next to Blynken. After checking his heart, eyes, and ears, he locked gazes with Martha.

"Has he been grinding his teeth?"

"I don't know. He's been chewing on something."

Dr. Goodrich checked Blynken's mouth as Martha had done, then began feeling the little goat's stomach. After a few minutes of studying, he rose to his feet and brushed off his knees.

"Do you know what's wrong?" asked Martha.

"I certainly do, and frankly, I'm surprised you all haven't called me out here for this before. Blynken has a case of bloat. Very common in goats. I usually see cases of it in the spring though, not the fall, so this is unusual. See how his left side is bulging?" He pointed to the goat's stomach. Now that Dr. Goodrich mentioned it, Martha could see that his stomach looked puffed up.

Dr. Goodrich continued. "He's grinding his teeth because he's in pain. And obviously, he's not eating, because his stomach feels overly full already."

Martha's heart ached, looking at the poor animal in the straw at their feet. "Will he be all right?"

Dr. Goodrich nodded. "I think he will, but we need to work quickly. Animals can die if this is left untreated. Has he had access to grass or grain lately?"

Martha filled him in on the particulars of Blynken's diet, and Dr. Goodrich retrieved some items from his truck before getting to work. He filled a syringe with some kind of oil and squirted it into Blynken's mouth. The goat stopped his grinding for a few seconds to lap at the oil.

"Someone will need to check on him frequently until he improves. You'll need to massage his left side to move the gases out and try to get him walking as soon as possible. It will also help if you leave some baking soda out in a container for him to eat. That will aid in clearing up his digestion." He gave Martha a few additional instructions, which she cataloged away in her mind.

"I'll get Mary," Martha said. "She'll likely be the one watching over him as he recovers." She hoped her words predicting Blynken's improvement would prove to be true. She hated to see an animal confused and in pain. She stroked Blynken's head before walking out of the barn with the vet.

"Call me if you have questions," Dr. Goodrich said as he stuck out his hand to shake hers.

"Thanks so much," Martha said. She waved goodbye as the doctor climbed into his truck and pulled out of the lot.

Martha went back to the store and relayed Dr. Goodrich's instructions to her sisters.

Mary sighed. "I guess that means I need to cancel my date with Alex tonight."

"Don't do that," Elizabeth said. "We can all take shifts. You watch Blynken this afternoon, and I'll cover this evening so you can keep your dinner plans."

"I don't know," Mary said slowly. "What if he gets worse?"

Martha started to answer when Lillian Carstairs walked in the front door. She seemed much more upbeat than she had the last time she'd visited the store to sell her sentimental heirlooms.

"Lillian, what a pleasant surprise," Elizabeth said. "More items to sell?"

"No." Lillian smiled. "I was actually wondering if you still had the music box I brought in a few days ago."

"We do." Martha detected an edge of worry to Elizabeth's voice. "We didn't put it out to sell yet. I hope you didn't need the money right away?"

"No, no." Lillian waved her hands. "I don't need the money anymore."

Martha felt happy for the woman. "I take it that means you're doing better financially?"

"I certainly am." Lillian grinned ear to ear. "I met the most wonderful real estate agent. He's buying land in my area, and he's made a marvelous offer on my home and acreage. My money troubles are over. Instead of living in a small apartment by myself, I can afford to move into a senior complex in Lancaster with my sister. She says the grounds are beautiful. The residents have a garden to putter around in, and all sorts of activities to keep them occupied. More importantly, I'll be with my sister." She grinned. "It'll be like we're roomies in college."

"I'm happy for you," Martha said. "You're able to take some of your own possessions to your new place?"

"Some," said Lillian. "Especially small things like knick-knacks. I was checking to see if I could get the music box back. I realized soon after I let go of it that it did mean a great deal to me."

"Of course," Elizabeth said with a smile. "We had a feeling you might be back."

"I'd be happy to get it for you," Martha said. She hurried to the storeroom and brought the music box back to where Lillian waited. Martha set it on the counter and lifted the lid. The strains of "The Anniversary Waltz" filled the room. Once again, Martha felt her eyes well up as she thought of Chuck. As she watched the delicate china bird spinning in the center, she realized there was a chip out of the bird's beak. She pointed out the imperfection to Lillian. "I'm afraid there's some damage. We were very careful with it, but maybe it got bumped?"

"Oh, don't worry about that," Lillian said. "It's not anything you did. It's been like that for a long time. My oldest son dropped a toy on it when he was a toddler. It's funny to think about. He's nearing fifty now."

"Our mother used to remind us that time stops for no man," Elizabeth said.

"Isn't that the truth," Lillian agreed. "Anyway, I'm fine with the chip. Raymond always planned to get it fixed for one of our anniversaries, but he never got around to it."

Her eyes grew misty, and she waved a hand in front of her face, as if trying to keep her feelings at bay.

Martha understood precisely where Lillian was coming from. How many nights had she lain in bed, alone, aching for the sound of Chuck's footfall on the step as he came up from reading in the den? He'd always been such a night owl. Since he'd died, how many times had she put on a good front with friends and neighbors, smiling until her face felt like brittle, dried-out clay? The love of God and of people like her sisters, who cared about her, had rescued her from her loneliness.

Martha saw her own emotions etched all over Lillian's face, and her heart filled with compassion for the woman. She reached under the front counter for a tissue.

Lillian took it with a small smile as the tears rolled down her wrinkled cheeks. "Thank you."

"I lost my husband too. A little over three years ago."

Lillian sniffled and looked up. "You poor thing. What was his name?"

"Charles. Most everybody called him Chuck though." He'd been as fine a husband as she could have ever hoped for. Loyal, hardworking, steady. Chuck rarely complained, and he always made her feel as though she was the most special person in the room. She'd not only lost her husband when he died, she'd lost her best friend.

Elizabeth reached out and set a comforting hand on Martha's shoulder, and Martha pressed her hand over her sister's in a gesture of gratitude. She hadn't spoken with many people, aside from her sisters, about Chuck. His loss had always seemed too close. Too present. But time really was healing her wounds. She'd never forget him or stop missing him, but now she could think about all the good times they'd shared throughout the years. Lillian would get to that point sometime too, but right now, she was suffering.

Martha silently handed Lillian another tissue, and the woman continued to dab at her face. Martha wished she could do something for Lillian. Something to make her feel cared for. Acknowledged.

Memories of Chuck swirled in her mind. He'd always been so good about making people feel cherished. An idea struck her. She rested a hand on the music box on the counter. "Why don't you let us fix it? We know of a shop where we could have it mended. If you can hold off for a few more days, we would be happy to get it repaired, free of charge, for you."

Lillian look so stunned, she almost stopped crying. "That is so kind of you. Thank you, that would be lovely."

"It's our pleasure," Elizabeth said. "We'll give you a call when it's ready. Or we can deliver it to your home."

"That would be wonderful," Lillian said. "It's so nice to have such sweet people helping me. First, that real estate agent offering to buy my house, then this. It's just answered prayers, I tell you. Answered prayers."

"It sounds like an answered prayer with how quickly things moved on your home," Martha said. "You said the real estate agent contacted you?"

"Yes." Lillian beamed. "Alan Keye. Of Keye Realty? Wonderful man. He not only sells properties but buys them too."

An image popped into Martha's mind. She exchanged a glance with Elizabeth and knew her sister was thinking the same thing. Wanda had mentioned seeing a suspicious man in the café. The Amish farmer had witnessed a car with a key on its side in the parking lot where Darlene disappeared. Could this be the third customer in the café that night?

Alan Keye. Was he the man who abducted Darlene? Were they finally close to finding her?

CHAPTER TWENTY-FIVE

"A re you sure I shouldn't stay and help you with Blynken?" Mary asked again. She was trying not to feel guilty about leaving the little guy.

Elizabeth, who was seated at the kitchen table going over the day's receipts, frowned at her. "No, Mary. Alex will be here any minute. Besides, Blynken is doing much better. He's not so bloated, and he's starting to eat. I think he'll be perfectly fine by morning."

"You know, I remember Mama saying something about one of the goats going through something like this," Martha said. "Just can't remember which one. Dr. Goodrich said it's common with goats."

Mary shook her head. "Well, it may be common, but I hate seeing Blynken in pain. He's such a sweetheart. He runs to meet me every morning when I come out to feed them. Wynken and Nod are a little more standoffish. I think they're beginning to come around though."

"They might still miss Mama," Elizabeth said. "She certainly loved them."

"I believe they loved her too." Mary sighed. "All right, I guess I'll go."

Martha removed a casserole from the oven and then turned around to look at Elizabeth. "You need to call John about that real estate agent. Alan Keye. He might be our guy."

Elizabeth's eyebrows shot up. "Just because he might have a key on the side of his car doesn't mean he's done anything wrong."

"He may have been the one driving back and forth near Heinrich and Faith's house," Martha said. "Pretty unusual behavior."

Elizabeth sighed loudly. "But that's not enough to suspect him of kidnapping Darlene. What motive does he have? Why would he kidnap a waitress and hold her for so long?"

"I realize that, but John could at least check up on him."

"I'll call him," Elizabeth said, "but I'm not sure what he can do except to ask Mr. Keye a few questions."

"I wish Clyde would file a missing person report," Martha said, exasperation in her voice.

Elizabeth shrugged. "We can't force him to do it, but maybe we should approach him about it again. Why don't you tell him the truth, Martha? That you think you saw his daughter being abducted. Maybe then he'll file that report."

Martha shook her head slowly. "I don't think his health is very good, and I worry that the shock of hearing that his daughter might have been kidnapped could be detrimental."

"But if something worse happens, Martha, wouldn't that affect him more?"

Elizabeth's soft response seemed to strike Martha, who paused and stared at her for a moment. "You might be right," she said. "I hadn't thought about it quite like that." She straightened her shoulders and grabbed two plates out of the nearby cabinet. "If something doesn't happen soon, I'll talk to him again." She put the plates down next to the casserole dish and gazed at her sisters. "It's been almost a week. I'm so worried about Darlene."

Her voice caught, and Mary felt the urgency Martha was experiencing. She was right. They needed to push harder to find Darlene. But right now Mary couldn't do anything about it. She pushed her concerns aside to concentrate on her date with Alex.

She looked down at the dark blue dress she'd chosen for her date. "Does this look okay?" she asked.

"It's lovely," Elizabeth said with a smile. "And you did something different with your hair."

"It's getting a little long. I really need to get it cut." Mary touched her head. She'd swept her hair up and fastened it with a deep blue antique rhinestone pin that had belonged to their mother. It matched the dress.

"You look perfect, Mary," Martha said. "You'll knock his socks off."

For some reason, Mary's stomach tightened. Was she just nervous? "Thanks," she said, taking a deep breath to relax.

"Where are you going?" Martha asked.

"Some new French restaurant in Lancaster," Mary said.

Martha's eyebrows shot up. "French? Do you like French food?"

Mary nodded. "Brian liked it. We had a favorite restaurant…." Her voice trailed off. She didn't want to talk about Brian. Frankly, going to a French restaurant reminded her of him. She wished they were going somewhere else, but Alex seemed excited about this place. "Paradou," she said suddenly.

"What?" Elizabeth asked.

"The name of the restaurant. I just remembered it."

"Oh." Elizabeth got up from her chair and went over to where Mary leaned against the kitchen counter. She took Mary's hands in hers. "Are you all right?" she asked.

Mary was surprised to feel tears spring to her eyes. "I guess so. I don't know what's wrong with me. I've been feeling uneasy all day. It's probably because of Blynken. I've been so concerned about him. He's such a darling little thing."

Elizabeth gave Mary a hug. When she let her go, she gazed into her eyes. "There might be more to what you're feeling, but you'll have to sort it out yourself, Mary."

"What do you mean?"

Elizabeth shrugged. "All I can tell you is to pray and believe God will guide you in the right direction."

Mary was getting ready to ask her once more what she was talking about when car headlights swept across the house. Alex. Mary picked up the cream-colored shawl she'd chosen to wear from the back of a chair at the kitchen table and tossed it over her shoulders. She was reaching for a small clutch purse that matched the shawl when the doorbell rang.

Pal, who was lying under the kitchen table, started barking, something he usually never did. He was used to people coming into the store—and the house. Tink, their little dachshund who was stretched out next to Pal, scooted out and walked away as if embarrassed by the border collie.

"Pal, hush," Martha said in a commanding voice.

Pal immediately looked crestfallen and slunk up next to her, causing Martha to laugh. "It's okay," she told him. She looked at Mary. "I think he was asleep, and the bell startled him."

"Are you through?" Mary asked, smiling at the dog, whose tail began to wag. Mary chuckled and opened the door. Alex stood there, wearing a black suit and a blue tie that matched Mary's dress. He stepped into the kitchen, a smile on his face.

He gestured at Mary's dress. "I guess great minds think alike," he said, his smile growing wider. "We match."

"You're an impressive-looking couple," Elizabeth said as she sat back down at the table. "Perfect for…what was the name of the restaurant?"

"Paradou," Alex said. "I think it's the owner's name. I've been told good things about it, but I've never been there."

"Well, something else we have in common," Mary said. "I hadn't even heard of it until you mentioned it."

Alex frowned. "I hope you like French food. I should have checked with you first. We can go somewhere else if you want."

Mary smiled at him. "I'm looking forward to it. I love French food. Are you ready to go?"

He said goodbye to Martha and Elizabeth and held the door open for her.

Mary waved at her sisters and stepped out into a beautiful September evening. She loved the start of fall. The leaves turning, a slight nip in the air, and an expectation of pumpkins and bonfires. She breathed it in and took Alex's offered arm. They went down the steps, and Mary got into his car, Alex holding the door open for her and closing it after she was safely seated. He was a true gentleman.

It didn't take long to get to the restaurant, and they filled the silence with small talk. Mary was pretty sure Alex was feeling a little tension as well. Their first date. Would there be more?

When they arrived at the restaurant, Mary was immediately impressed. It was housed in a light blue building with wood siding, large glass windows, and a walkway built with wooden slats leading to a large, whitewashed carved door. Small golden twinkle lights were strung overhead, creating an almost magical ambience. Something about the way the restaurant looked seemed oddly familiar, but that couldn't be right. Mary was certain she'd never been there before.

As they entered, they were greeted by a hostess who checked their reservation and led them into a large dining room. The tables were covered with white tablecloths and candles that twinkled in the muted lighting.

"What do you think?" Alex whispered as they followed the hostess to a table in the corner of the room, near a lit fireplace. The flame was so low it didn't produce much heat, but it certainly added to the charm of the room. Looking closer, Mary realized the logs weren't real, although it was hard to tell the difference, and the fireplace was gas, not wood burning. As Alex held out her chair, Mary felt that everything was perfect. The restaurant, the table, and the handsome man who sat down across from her. She pushed away the nerves that had dogged her all afternoon, ever since Alex asked her out. It was stupid, and she had no plans to allow feelings that made no sense to ruin this wonderful evening.

An impeccably dressed waiter came to the table and took their drink orders while Mary perused the menu. She had just decided on the charbroiled chicken with seasoned rice and white wine sauce, when she heard a familiar voice say hello.

She looked up to see Bill standing next to the table, staring down at her. At that moment she realized why so many aspects of the building looked familiar.

"You…you helped build this restaurant, didn't you?" she asked. "I recognize your work."

"I only added some touches. The door, the counter in the front, and the walkway. And we painted the outside. I'm here to give the owner a bid for some benches in the front. They'd like something a little more decorative than what's there now."

"I'm sure you can improve it," Mary said. "Everything is lovely." She swallowed hard and looked at Alex, who hadn't said anything. "Alex, do you know—"

"Of course we know each other," Alex said. "Went to school together. How are you, Billy? It's been a long time." Alex stuck out his hand, and Bill took it.

"It has been a while. And it's Bill now."

After shaking hands, Bill said, "I don't want to bother you. Just wanted to say hello." He gazed into Mary's eyes for a moment and then turned and walked away. Mary felt something like a jolt of electricity move through her. And for the first time she realized why she'd felt edgy all day. It was time to face the truth. Elizabeth's words drifted into her mind. *All I can tell you is to pray and believe God will guide you in the right direction.*

Elizabeth had been right. She felt God speaking to her heart. She had deep feelings for Bill Richmond, and they were a lot more than just friendship.

CHAPTER TWENTY-SIX

How was Blynken doing when you checked on him?" Martha asked Mary the next morning as she entered Secondhand Blessings. To her surprise, Mary didn't answer her question. She just drifted into her spot behind the counter with a daydreamy look on her face.

"Mary?"

Still no response. Mary stared off into space as though a movie only she could see was playing in her mind.

Martha didn't want to be rude, but she did want to know how Blynken was, as well as find out why Mary was so unfocused. She waved her hand in front of her sister's face. "Are you all right?"

At the motion, Mary blinked and frowned at her sister. "What? I'm fine."

Martha made a face at her. "Are you? You seem…distracted. I asked you how Blynken was, and it was like you didn't even hear me."

"Oh." Mary seemed nonplussed. "Blynken's doing better. He's up and walking now. Dr. Goodrich thinks he'll be back to normal in a few days. I'm so glad we caught what was wrong with him in time."

"I am too," Martha agreed. "Is that what you've been thinking about? Blynken?"

"Maybe a little." Mary leaned closer to her sister and lowered her voice. "But I'm mostly thinking about my date last night with Alex."

"How was it? I was so tired that I went to bed before you got home. We didn't get a chance to talk."

"It should have been wonderful." Mary sighed. "The restaurant was beautiful, Martha, all decorated with candles and lights. The food was delicious. Alex was—" She paused, as if searching for the right words.

"Alex was—what?"

Mary took a deep breath. "Alex was very nice…."

"I sense there's more to that sentence than you're letting on."

"But…" Mary took another deep breath. "He wasn't Bill."

It was all Martha could do to keep from cheering out loud. Finally! She'd played along with Elizabeth's gentle teasing of Mary over Alex Wright, but everyone knew that Mary belonged with Bill. It had just taken her a long time to come around to it. The intense look in Mary's eyes told Martha that this focus on Bill was serious, and Martha couldn't be happier. "I'm glad you've realized that, Mary. Bill Richmond is a fine man."

"He is, isn't he?" Mary asked. Her eyes assumed that far-off, wistful look again.

Martha started to ask a question, but just then, Elizabeth hurried out of the office, where she'd been taking a phone call. "I've got news, girls."

Mary didn't look up at Elizabeth's presence and continued to stare dreamily into space.

"Is she all right?" Elizabeth asked.

"She's fine. Bitten by the lovebug, it seems."

"Not Alex?" Elizabeth's face fell. "I didn't think she'd take me seriously. I was only teasing about him."

"No." Martha couldn't help but grin. "It's Bill."

"Bill?" Elizabeth's eyes lit up, and she threw her arms around Mary. "It's about time! We've known you two were a good match forever. I'm glad you've finally jumped on board with the idea too." She pulled away from Mary. "So, tell us what happened. Did he ask you out on a date?"

Mary's smile froze. "No. Not yet. He showed up when I was at Paradou with Alex, and the moment I saw him, it was like things finally clicked into place. I realized Bill is the only guy for me. But he doesn't know I feel differently now, so why would he ask me out?"

"You'll have to tell him how you feel," Martha said.

"I don't know," Mary said slowly.

"He deserves to know, Mary," Elizabeth said. "He's been very open with how he feels about you. Don't let a misunderstanding keep you two apart."

"I guess you're right." Mary smiled at them. "What would I do without my sisters and their good advice?" She paused, as though the haze had cleared from her mind. "Wait a minute, did you say you had news?"

Elizabeth cleared her throat. "Right. I just got off the phone with John, and he said he was able to talk with Denver Carlton. Denver's trial ended this morning. His side won the case."

"What does it have to do with finding Darlene?"

Elizabeth leaned onto her elbows on the counter. "Because Denver was finally straight with John. It turns out, he had been at the Two Bird recently."

"Then why didn't he tell John the truth?" Martha asked.

"A witness from the defense tried to talk to him at the restaurant," Elizabeth continued. "But he refused. He didn't want their chance encounter to spark a mistrial, if word got out."

"What about Alan Keye?"

Elizabeth sighed. "John is going to try to track him down today. He's the only suspect left on our list, other than Arnold. I wonder if we should visit Darlene's father today and fill him in on what's going on. I know you're concerned about him, but I don't see what other choice we have. He's Darlene's father, and he deserves to know his daughter may in trouble."

Martha knew Elizabeth was right. "I can do that this afternoon. I planned to drop that music box of Lillian's off at the jeweler's anyway."

"Perfect. I know you've been worried about Darlene, Martha, but I think we're close to figuring out what's happened. She's going to be home safe very soon."

Martha wished she felt as confident as Elizabeth sounded, but they were doing all they could. They just had to keep moving forward.

Up to that point, Mary hadn't participated in the conversation at all, but her head snapped up as soon as a customer walked through the sliding doors of the shop. Not just any customer though. Bill Richmond's familiar form strode across the room to the front counter. Martha watched with interest to see what Mary's reaction would be.

Bill looked about as dazed as Mary. He ran a hand through his hair, which was uncharacteristically ruffled and messy. His features wore an expression of pure misery. Martha didn't know if she had ever seen the man in such a state before. Bill was normally so calm and composed.

"Hello, Bill. What can we help you with today?" Elizabeth greeted him, but he didn't answer her question. He just made an unintelligible sound that sounded like a half-hearted greeting. Then he turned his full attention to Mary.

"We need to talk."

"Now?" Mary looked startled.

Bill's ears turned red. He tried to talk but faltered. Finally, he got some words out. "I'm—I mean, only if you're not busy. I mean—I'd like to talk to you alone—" He broke off the sentence.

Mary clearly took pity on him. "I guess I can talk to you now." She glanced at Elizabeth and Martha for confirmation, and they both nodded. Bill stepped aside to let Mary walk ahead of him to the front doors, then he followed her. For the fraction of a second, Martha saw him lift his hand toward her back as though to guide her outside, but he dropped it before he actually touched her. Mary headed out the door, oblivious to his small action.

Martha smiled at Elizabeth. Was Mary going to tell Bill about her feelings for him?

Mary's heart raced, and her palms sweated as she headed in the direction of the parking lot, with Bill close behind her.

What was he going to talk to her about? He was acting so nervous that it made her feel jittery.

Bill motioned toward his truck. "It's a little chilly out today. We could sit in the cab to talk if you want."

A breeze ruffled Mary's hair. It was cooler today than it had been earlier in the week. "Okay." She climbed into his truck, even though her heart pounded wildly in her ears at the thought of being in even closer proximity to Bill. This was silly. She'd been nervous around him before, but never like this. Then again, she'd never known with certainty before how she felt about him. Now she had something to lose.

She shut the door. Poor Bill looked like a kid getting ready to present a speech at school assembly. His behavior was boyishly cute, and she felt her nerves dissipate a little as she fully realized that he must feel the same way she did. He took a deep breath. "Mary, I've been thinking about something since I saw you last night at Paradou—"

Mary jumped in. "I've been thinking about something since then too."

He held his hand up to stop her. "Now, Mary, let me get this off my chest first." He had a determined look in his eye, so she let him speak. "I feel the same way about you as I always have. I like you, Mary. I have since we were kids, and I think that you like me too, whether or not you're dating Alex. I know he's a nice guy and I should be happy because you're happy, but to tell the truth, Mary, I just thought that if you were really ready to date anyone, it wouldn't be him. It would be—"

"Bill!" Mary couldn't stay silent. "I'm not interested in Alex."

He blinked. "You're not? You were on a date with him."

Mary nodded. "I was, but as soon as I saw you, I knew that as nice as Alex was, he wasn't the one I wanted sitting across the table from me." She held her breath. She felt as if she had just flung herself off the high dive and was preparing for the exhilarating crash into the water. She hadn't put her heart on the line for anyone since Brian had left her. She'd had a few short relationships, if you could even call them that. But she'd never let anyone get close. Until now. "I sat there wishing it was you, Bill."

"Do you really mean that?" Bill looked a bit shocked, as though he hadn't prepared for her response after his speech.

"Yes. I feel the same way you do, and I'm ready for our relationship to be more than friendship."

The slow grin that spread across Bill's face told her everything she needed to know. He took her hands in his and said the words she'd prayed to hear.

"Mary, would you go to dinner with me tonight?"

His hands felt steady and comfortable on hers. As frightening as it was to take the leap into a real relationship, she also felt joy bubble up inside of her. Bill was not Brian. He was different, and he'd proven himself over and over throughout the years to be kind. Loyal.

He waited for her answer, letting her take her time and make her decision. Finally, she grinned back at him.

"I can't think of anything I'd like more."

CHAPTER TWENTY-SEVEN

Martha smiled when Mary came back into the shop. She beamed with happiness.

"Your talk must have gone well," Martha said.

"Very well," Elizabeth added. "Tell us, tell us."

Before Mary had a chance to say anything, the front doors slid open, and Arnold walked in, his grubby knit cap pulled down low, almost covering his eyes. Elizabeth got up from the stool behind the counter and met him before he got too far inside. Martha came up behind her in case she needed help.

"I...I'm sorry to bother you ladies," he said gruffly, "but you said you could take things on consignment?" He blinked several times. "I need money real bad." He reached into his pocket and pulled out the watch he'd brought in before. "Can I leave this here? On consignment, I mean?"

Martha saw Elizabeth's expression change from suspicion to compassion. Not surprising. That was Elizabeth. A big heart, to be sure.

"Why don't you bring your watch over here?" Elizabeth suggested, gesturing toward the front counter. "Let me take a closer look at it."

Martha started to say something, but Elizabeth put her finger to her lips after the man turned around. All she could do was watch as Elizabeth looked more closely at the watch.

"This is a very nice watch," she said. "I think we can get a good price for it." She hesitated a moment. "Why don't I advance you a little bit on it? I'm sure I can make the money back."

Arnold, who had come in looking like a whipped dog, brightened visibly. "That would be great. Thank you very much, ma'am."

While Elizabeth wrote out a ticket for the watch, Mary went over to the shelves where they kept their baked goods and jams. She got a bag and put some loaves of bread and a couple of jars of jam inside it. Then she carried it over to Arnold. She handed it to him without saying a word.

"Thank you. You're very kind," he said. "I know that policeman doesn't want me here, so I won't bother you much longer." He reached for a pen and pad of paper on the counter where he quickly wrote something down. "This is my number...for now. If it changes, I'll let you know." For the first time, he actually smiled. "I hope you get a lot for the watch." He looked down at it and the smile slipped from his face. "It belonged to my father. He got it from my grandfather. I hate to sell it, but... Well, I don't have much choice."

Elizabeth looked at the piece of paper Arnold had signed. Then she opened the cash register and took out some money. She handed it to him. "Here's an advance of seventy-five dollars. I know your watch is worth much more, so when it sells, I'll call you to come get the rest."

Arnold held up his hand. "I'm grateful for this. Thank you." His eyes swept across the sisters. "I truly appreciate your generosity." He hung his head for a moment. "I haven't always been like this, you know. I used to be...successful. But I made some bad choices and ruined my life. Lost my job, my home, my family. Things I'll never get back."

Mary reached over and touched the man's well-worn jacket. "God can turn everything around, Arnold. Our church has some resources that could help you. Perhaps you could—"

"No." Arnold's response cut off Mary's words. "I'm just not into God. Sorry. I'm sure you believe, but I just don't. Not after everything that's happened to me."

"If you change your mind, please contact Mount Zion Mennonite Church," Mary said. "They're very willing to help."

Arnold put the money in his pocket and picked up the bag Mary had given him. "Thank you again." With that, he hurried out the front doors.

"You gave him seventy-five dollars?" Martha asked. "What if the watch doesn't sell?"

Elizabeth leveled her gaze at her sister. "Do you think I was wrong?"

Martha took a deep breath and let it out slowly. "No," she said. "I think you reached out to provide assistance to someone in need. We're supposed to help people. But some folks can't be helped, Lizzie. John warned us about this guy. What if he keeps coming back, asking for money?"

"It's a chance we'll have to take," she said. "I couldn't turn him away. I get the feeling he's just someone down on his luck. He mentioned that something happened that put him where he is." She sighed. "I'll tell John what we did. I doubt he'll be happy about it."

180 | MYSTERIES of LANCASTER COUNTY

"Now, if we're done talking about Arnold," Martha said, fastening her eyes on Mary, "can we find out what you and Bill talked about outside?"

Mary's eyes shone. "Well, let's just say that we're going out tonight."

"Is that it?" Martha asked.

Mary's smile spread slowly across her face. "We admitted that we care about each other. More than just friends do. Is that what you wanted to hear?"

Elizabeth laughed. "Yes, I guess it is."

"What about Alex?" Martha asked.

"He's such a nice man," Mary said with a sigh. "But he's just not the right man for me. There's nothing wrong with him, but I feel different about Bill." She shook her head. "I intend to take it slow. After Brian, I need to be careful. Of course, at one time I would have told you that Brian would never cheat on me. I wonder if we ever really know people."

"But you've known Bill since you were both kids," Elizabeth said. "By now, I think you've learned that he's not Brian. Bill is as rock steady as they come."

"He is, isn't he?"

"He really is," Martha said. She reached over and hugged Mary. "I'm so happy for you."

"Thank you." She let go of Martha and gazed into her eyes. "Not everyone married a Chuck. I know you miss him, but what a blessing it must have been to be loved that much."

Martha felt tears spring to her eyes. "You're right. I did feel blessed. I can only pray that someday you'll have what I had."

This time Mary's eyes filled with tears, and she gave Martha another quick hug. As Martha released her, a large clap of thunder shook the shop and the sound of rain hit the roof.

Martha frowned. "I was going to take that music box to the jewelry store so they could fix the bird's beak, but I hate to drive in a downpour."

"Well, at least we're not busy," Elizabeth said. "When it rains, business seems to fall off quite a bit."

"You're right," Martha said. She searched under the counter and found the box they'd put the music box in. She put it on top of the counter as Mary went over to the doors and looked outside.

"It's not that bad," she said. "Seems to be a steady rain, but not as bad as it sounded."

"Good." Martha picked up the box and got her raincoat and umbrella. "I want to get Horace working on this as soon as possible." Horace Comstock owned Comstock Jewelry Store. He was a talented jeweler and had repaired many pieces for them. Martha had high hopes he could replace the bird's broken beak.

She said goodbye to her sisters and hustled to her car. It really wasn't too bad, although dark clouds moving across the sky looked somewhat ominous. She carefully put the box in the passenger seat and slid the key into the ignition. It took a couple of attempts to get the car started. Once again, the oil light came on. She really had to take her car into the garage. Looking for Darlene had taken up so much of her time that she'd kept putting off whatever repairs were needed.

She was still a few miles from the jewelry store in Lancaster when her engine suddenly began to knock loudly. Alarmed by the way the car shook, Martha looked on both sides of the street for a place to stop. She couldn't believe her luck when she saw a car repair shop coming up. She turned into the lot just as her car died. She tried to start it again, but there was no sound when she turned the key. She had passed Morton's Auto Repair many times, but she'd never taken her car there because there was a good shop closer to home. The place seemed busy most of the time, which gave Martha hope that they were skilled at what they did. She got her purse and hurried into the shop. A man stood behind a counter, talking on the phone. When he saw her, he hung up.

"What can I do for you?" he asked, his eyebrows knit together in a scowl.

Martha pointed toward her car. "Something's wrong. The oil light's been on a while. Then it started knocking and stopped. Can you look at it?"

The man seemed to hesitate a moment. "I...I guess so. We can't get to it until later today though. Maybe tomorrow. Can you leave it here?" He pushed a clipboard toward her. "Please fill out this form. We need your contact information."

Martha pulled the clipboard closer, picked up the pen he handed her, and quickly wrote down her name, address, and phone number. Then she handed him her car keys. "I need to call my sister to come and get me."

The man, whose shirt was embroidered with the name Bart, pointed at a couple of old chairs sitting against the wall. "You can wait there."

He walked away, leaving Martha standing alone. As he moved her car from outside into the bay, the man seemed distracted. Odd. She sighed as she sat down in one of the rickety chairs. Then she took out her phone and called Elizabeth. As she waited for her to answer, she wondered when she'd become so suspicious of everyone. It was getting to be ridiculous. But even though she tried to reassure herself everything was okay, she couldn't rid herself of a strange feeling of apprehension.

CHAPTER TWENTY-EIGHT

Secondhand Blessings, this is Elizabeth." Elizabeth's voice filled the receiver. Martha relaxed in her chair and breathed a sigh of relief.

"Thank goodness I reached you. My car broke down."

Elizabeth gasped. "Are you all right?"

"I'm fine. I happened to be passing by an auto shop when the engine died, and I was able to swing into the lot. Can you pick me up at Morton's Auto Repair?" She gave Elizabeth directions then disconnected the call and slipped her phone into her open purse. If the jeweler's was closer, she could walk there and drop off the music box before Elizabeth arrived. But it was too far. Maybe Elizabeth would swing by on the way back to the store. It would only take a few minutes.

She had to retrieve the music box and umbrella from her car first though. In all the flurry of activity with the car breaking down, she'd forgotten them. She walked up to the counter where Bart stood scribbling information on a ticket pad. He didn't look up at her until she cleared her throat loudly.

"I was wondering if I could get in my car. I left some things inside that I need."

Bart narrowed his eyes. Was he seriously going to say no? To her relief, he finally shrugged. He followed her back to her car, as if she was going to steal something. Her umbrella was still dripping wet, but she looped the strap over her wrist anyway and then leaned over to retrieve the music box. She'd carefully wrapped it in bubble wrap so as not to incur any more damages. As she bent over, her purse swung off her shoulder onto the floorboard. Several items fell out. She scooped them up quickly and shoved them back into her purse. Bart side-eyed her as she retrieved it and straightened with the music box in her grip.

"Is that all you needed?" he asked gruffly.

"Yes, thank you."

He led her back to the reception area, where she waited for a short time until Elizabeth appeared.

"That was quick," Martha said.

Elizabeth shrugged. "I made good time. Mary is watching the shop. There were hardly any customers when I left, so she should be okay for a while. We do need to get back soon though. She'll want some time to get ready for her date tonight."

"She did seem pretty excited about going out with Bill." Martha grinned. That was the understatement of the year.

"I'm so glad she's finally ready to see him," Elizabeth said. "Bill is kind and steady, exactly the kind of man she needs. I can't think of anyone else I'd be happier to see her date."

"He's a good man," Martha agreed. "And the most important part is that he seems to make Mary genuinely happy."

Elizabeth smiled. "I agree." She looped her arm through Martha's as they walked out the door and to her car. Within a few minutes, they'd arrived at Comstock Jewelry Store. Horace Comstock greeted them warmly. Martha filled him in on the repairs the music box needed, and he assured them that he'd have the piece looking good as new by Monday. The sisters thanked him and left.

If only every problem were so easy to fix. Martha had been distracted the majority of the day, thinking about Lillian, Arnold, and her broken-down car. Now that those things were resolved, her thoughts turned to Darlene again. They'd hit a brick wall with almost all their suspects, and the police still weren't involved in the search. Martha sent up a prayer for Darlene's safety. It felt like the only thing left that she could do for her.

Mary sat at the counter of Secondhand Blessings, impatiently waiting for her sisters to return. She kept an eye trained on the clock. 4:46. Where were Elizabeth and Martha? They'd been gone for a long time. She drummed her fingers on the countertop. The minutes ticked by until it was after five. With a sigh, she finished closing up the shop and went back to the house to start getting ready for her date. At five thirty, her sisters finally pulled up outside in Elizabeth's SUV.

"Sorry," Martha said as she entered the house, shaking raindrops from her umbrella. "We had to make a quick stop on the way home."

"It's okay," Mary said. She'd changed her outfit four times already. Bill hadn't given her any indication where they were going for dinner, so she wasn't sure how to dress. She wanted to look nice but not like she was trying too hard. It was a fine line to walk.

"Mary, you look lovely!" Elizabeth set her purse down and crossed the room.

"Oh, this old thing?" Mary grinned and smoothed down her lace-edged blouse. "I'm a little nervous."

"Don't be silly. There's no reason to be nervous." Martha was reassuring in her own no-nonsense way. "You've known Bill for years. My only question is, what will you find to talk about? You know everything about each other's lives already."

"I doubt that," Elizabeth said. "Rachel was just telling me the other day that she discovered Silas dislikes schnitz pies. He doesn't like dried apples, but since he eats other desserts with apples, Rachel had no idea. You know how long they've been married." She smiled in Mary's direction. "Just try to relax and enjoy the evening. We'll be excited to hear all about it when you get home."

Mary let out a long breath. "All right." She wished she felt as calm as her sisters encouraged her to be.

Outside, the faint noise of an approaching car hinted at Bill's arrival. Then headlights shone across the windows. Mary dabbed on a tiny bit of lipstick and hugged Elizabeth and Martha goodbye, grateful for their support. It had been a long road the past few years, getting over Brian's rejection and finding herself worthy of love again. Through it all, her family—and God—had never abandoned her. No matter how things went with Bill tonight, it would all be okay.

A knock sounded at the door. Feeling more secure, Mary answered it. Bill stood on the porch, dressed nicely in a pair of dark jeans and a collared dress shirt. His grin made her heart beat a little faster.

"You look beautiful." He extended a hand to help her down the porch steps. "Ready to go?"

A blush warmed her cheeks, but she happily took his hand. Any nerves she had left faded as she walked beside him, though she wasn't certain he felt quite as at ease as she did. Once inside his truck, Bill fiddled with the dials, adjusting the flow of air.

"Is the temperature all right?" He held his hand in front of an air vent to test it. "If it's too warm, I can change it. Or too cold."

Mary smiled. "I'm fine."

"Are you sure? Because I can adjust it so it comes out at the floorboards too."

Mary just shook her head. It was funny seeing Bill like this. She'd known him for so long, and he'd always been so laid back. She didn't want him to feel nervous, but she was kind of flattered he cared so much about her comfort.

"What about music? Would you like to listen to anything?" Bill ran a hand through his previously neat hair. "I'm sorry to say I don't even know what kind of music you like. Not a ton of signal out here, so most of the stations are fuzzy...." He toyed with the controls again and flipped though stations quicker than Mary could distinguish between them.

"I think that one's country.... This one might be classical, though it's hard to tell with all the static. I could leave it on this one as we drive into town, and the sound might clear up—"

"Bill." Mary placed a hand over his. "You're fine. I'm fine. Don't worry so much."

She was relieved to see his tense posture relax slightly.

"I've just been waiting a long time to take you out on an official first date, Mary, and I want this to go well."

She smiled at him again. "Trust me. If we're together, it will be a wonderful evening."

CHAPTER TWENTY-NINE

Mary had to admit, she was surprised by Bill's choice of restaurant. It wasn't that the Olympic Diner wasn't a good place to eat. Their burgers, fries, and hand-dipped milkshakes were some of the best in Lancaster. Her mouth watered just thinking about it. The place even sported an old-fashioned soda fountain along the back wall.

She wasn't upset that he'd picked the Olympic for their first official date, but it was just a bit more...casual than she had expected. She'd envisioned a replay of Paradou, except with Bill across the table from her this time, as it should be. She struggled to square a burger joint with her expectations.

Her confused expression must have shown, because Bill's face fell. "You're disappointed."

"No, no," she was quick to assure him. The last thing she wanted was for him to feel bad. She really didn't mind where they ate, as long as she was with him. "The food is so good here. I can't wait to order."

"You were expecting something fancier, weren't you?"

How had he read her mind? "I think I was picturing some place more like Paradou. Maybe because we were both there the other day."

"That's a good restaurant. A classic first date place," Bill agreed. "But it's kind of impersonal. I wanted to choose a location that had meaning behind it. History."

She felt blank. "And the Olympic has...history?" It was a family business that had been in operation even before she was born. A lot of the fixtures inside, like the impressive soda fountain, were original. Was that what he meant?

Bill smiled. "It has history for us. Do you remember coming here when we were kids?"

Mary searched her mind, trying to recall if she'd visited the diner with Bill sometime in the past. "I'm sorry. I remember coming here when I was in high school, but we never met here. Did we?"

Bill chuckled. "We never came here together. But I was sitting with my buddies in that booth over there"—he pointed across the room—"when I first realized I had a crush on you. I told myself that if we ever had a first date, this would be the place I'd take you. But then you and Brian started dating. When you got married and moved away, I put that old dream on a shelf."

"Until now."

"Yes." Bill's eyes shone. "Until now."

A waitress appeared to seat them.

"Do you mind if we sit over there?" Bill asked, motioning toward the booth he'd pointed out to Mary. "For old time's sake?"

"Of course." The waitress led them to the booth, and Mary slid into one side with Bill across the table from her.

Mary silently thanked God for mended hopes and second chances. Maybe falling in love again was possible. But this time she wanted it to be forever. Was Bill the man who could fulfill her dreams?

"What can I get you to drink?" the waitress asked.

Mary looked at her name badge. DEBBIE. "I'll take a root beer float," she said. "Thank you, Debbie."

The young woman, who looked to be somewhere around eighteen or twenty, smiled. "You're welcome." She turned to Bill. "And for you, sir?" she asked.

Bill grinned widely at Mary. "I'll have the same, Debbie. Thanks."

"You're welcome. I'll be right back with those...and some menus."

As Debbie walked away, Bill said, "You're a very nice person, Mary. Do you know that?"

Mary frowned at him. "Why? Because I looked at the waitress's name?"

"Most people don't care. They just want their food. The person who serves it to them is invisible."

"I just remembered. You worked here for a while, didn't you?"

Bill nodded. "And every time you came in, I made sure you got an extra scoop of ice cream in your root beer float."

Mary's mouth dropped open. "I used to show people my float and point out the extra ice cream. We all thought it was an accident. It didn't happen every time."

"Because I only worked three days a week." Bill laughed.

Mary giggled. "I love root beer floats. Can't get them in a lot of restaurants."

"I know. It's a shame."

Mary had opened her mouth to say something else when the door to the diner opened, and Arnold Kopeckni came in. He stumbled as the door closed behind him, and he grabbed the coatrack to steady himself.

"Is something wrong?" Bill asked.

"The man who just came in," Mary whispered. "He's been hanging around town. And our shop. John says he's bad news. You know, I think he's drunk." She looked away as Arnold's eyes swept over the dining area. He finally trudged over to the counter and sat down, his back to them.

Bill turned to his left until he could see Arnold. "He looks down on his luck."

"That's what we thought," Mary said. "But John's pretty insistent we stay away from him." She sighed. "I keep wondering if..." She stopped as she realized Bill didn't know about Darlene's disappearance.

"What were you wondering?" he asked.

Just then, Debbie brought their root beer floats. She put them on the table and handed each of them a menu. She bent over the table a bit to catch Mary's eye.

"I noticed you looking at that guy," she whispered. "Do you know him?"

"I know his name, but that's it," Mary answered.

"He's shown up here before wanting food. I think he's been drinking," Debbie said. "I can smell him from several feet away."

"Look, give him a good hot meal and some coffee," Bill said. "And put it on my tab. Make up some excuse why it's free."

"I'll tell him someone paid for an order but decided they didn't want it." She smiled. "It's the truth, isn't it?"

Bill laughed softly. "Yes, I suppose it is."

"I'll be back in a bit and get your orders."

Bill and Mary thanked her. After she walked away, Bill said, "You were getting ready to tell me something. Is it connected to this Arnold guy?"

"It's kind of a long story."

"I have time. Besides, I love to listen to you talk."

Mary knew she was blushing, but she didn't care. Her sisters had hinted more than once that sometimes she talked too much, but Bill never seemed to mind. She liked that about him.

She took a deep breath and told Bill about what Martha saw at the balloon festival. Then she went over all the things they'd done, trying to find Darlene.

"Shouldn't the police be looking for Darlene?" Bill asked.

"Sure, but why? Because Martha *might* have seen someone abducted? There's no proof. Even though he's not helping officially, John knows what's going on. He's doing what he can."

"Good." Bill frowned. "Why would anyone kidnap a waitress?"

"I don't know," Mary said. "That's what we're trying to find out. All we've had to go on are the people who were in the café when Darlene told her friend she overheard something she wasn't supposed to." She sighed. "So far we haven't been able to find a motive for any of them. But we're pretty sure one of them is involved."

"Wow. Must be tough. Seems to me that what her father said should make the investigation official. I mean, if Darlene doesn't have a sister. I find that alarming."

"Her father thinks she's just run off for a while," Mary said. "We haven't told him that we think she's been kidnapped."

"I see the problem." Bill eyed Arnold. "And you think this guy might be part of it?"

"We suspected him for a while. He used to date Darlene, but I don't think he had anything to do with her disappearance. John feels the same way. I think he's just a sad man down on his luck. John said he may be involved in illegal gambling, but they haven't been able to find out who's running it." Mary looked up to see Arnold weaving their way. She wasn't sure what to do. She caught Bill's eye and nodded toward the drunken man who was almost upon them. Bill turned around just as Arnold reached their booth.

"Hello, Arnold," Mary said. "How are you?"

Arnold leaned on the end of the table, obviously trying to keep himself upright. "That waitress told me someone didn't pay for a roast beef dinner. She asked me if I wanted it."

Actually, it sounded like he said, "roost bee dinner," but at the moment, Mary figured correcting him wasn't the priority. "That sounds nice," she said.

"I know you're trying to pay for my meal, but I don't need your help. I'll have money soon. Lots of money. You just wait and see." A little drool edged down his chin and into the hair on his unshaved face.

"Look, we're just trying to do something nice," Bill said, his voice firm but calm. "It's nothing to get upset about."

"I wasn't talkin' to you. You jes butt out, mister."

At that moment, the cook walked out of the back room. He came over and took Arnold by the arm. He looked over at Bill and Mary. "Sorry about this. He comes by sometimes and we give him food, but he's been told not to show up here when he's drunk." Then he addressed Arnold. "Come on. Time to go."

Arnold tried to wrestle away but couldn't disengage himself from the man's firm grip. The cook was at least six feet tall, beefy, and obviously strong. Arnold finally seemed to realize he wasn't going to win in a tussle with the man.

"But what about my food?" Arnold asked, his voice going up a notch. "I'm really hungry."

"You wait outside. We'll bring your food out."

"But it's cold out there," Arnold whined.

"Sorry, I'm not giving you any other choice. Say goodbye to your friends, and let's go."

"They're not my friends." He shook his head, then glared at Mary. "You're not so smart. I know things."

"That's it," the cook said. "Come on."

The cook hustled Arnold out the door and led him over to some tables set up for those who wanted to eat outside.

Mary sighed as she watched out the window. "I'm not sure why he's angry with me. We tried to help him."

"He's not upset with you," Bill said. "He's angry with himself. You were just in front of him. An easy target."

"You could be right."

The sound of a siren interrupted their conversation. A police car from the Lancaster Police Department pulled up and two officers got out. After speaking to Arnold for a few minutes, they got him up and into the back seat of their car. Debbie ran outside and handed them a Styrofoam box that probably held Arnold's "roost bee" dinner.

Mary shook her head as the patrol car pulled out of the parking lot. "Well, this has certainly been an interesting date. I hope there will be a second one."

"I wouldn't worry about that," Bill said with a wide smile. "I think we'll find time for many, many more."

Mary took a sip of her root beer float as her heart soared. Even with Arnold's interruption, this date was turning out to be the best one of her life.

As she drank her root beer float, she noticed Debbie coming toward their table. Mary smiled at her. "Thank you for dealing with Arnold. I appreciate it."

"You're welcome," she said. "That man...Arnold...he gave me a message for you." Debbie hesitated.

"It's all right," Mary said. "What's the message?"

Debbie took a deep breath. "He said he knows where the woman is."

CHAPTER THIRTY

Saturday morning, Martha and Mary opened the store while Elizabeth went to help Rachel at the variety stand. Mary had told Martha about her date with Bill once already and was repeating the same thing again. Martha smiled to herself. She was delighted to see how happy Mary was.

"If Arnold hadn't shown up, it would have been perfect," Mary said. "There for a little while, I thought maybe it was worth it. That maybe he knew how to find Darlene."

"John's call put an end to that," Martha said. "The police in Lancaster said Arnold can't remember saying that and has no idea where any *woman* is."

"Do you think he's telling the truth?"

"Unfortunately, I do," Martha said. "I think he said it in an attempt to upset you."

"He must've heard Bill and me talking about her." Mary shook her head. "It was an awful thing to do, but I still feel sorry for the man. He looks so sad."

"Lizzie said they were letting him go. They have nothing to hold him on, really."

Mary smiled. "Hey, sorry I've been going on and on about my date with Bill. Hope I didn't bore you."

Martha chuckled. "You're not boring me at all. I'm just pleased that you and Bill finally see eye to eye about your feelings for each other." Martha sat down behind the counter and prepared the cash register. "It's about time. He's been making big cow eyes at you since you were kids in school."

Mary straightened a row of embroidered dish towels and then stared at Martha. "I can't help but wonder what would have happened if we'd found each other in school. My life would have been so different."

"Yes, it would. You wouldn't have Michael or Jennifer."

Mary sighed. "Of course, you're right. I'd do things exactly the same way if changing things meant losing my kids." When she smiled at Martha, she had tears in her eyes. "They are the greatest blessing God has given me. My children...and my sisters. What would I do without you?"

It was Martha's turn to feel a little misty eyed. She dabbed at her eyes, then pointed at Mary. "Enough schmaltz. Let's get to work."

The morning got busy. Martha kept checking her phone, hoping the garage would call about her car. Besides worrying about that, she couldn't get Darlene out of her mind. It was now over a week since the balloon festival. Where was she? Were they too late to save her?

A little after ten, Autumn Guerrero and her daughter Carlie came into the store. Autumn had sold many things on consignment through Secondhand Blessings. When her mother died, she'd left behind a house full of items collected over the years. Too many things for Autumn to keep. She'd made quite a bit of money through the shop.

"Hi there," Autumn said to Martha when they came in.

"Hello." She smiled at Carlie. "How are you?" The six-year-old slipped behind her mother and smiled shyly at Martha.

Autumn gently took Carlie's arm and guided her out of her hiding place. "Tell Mrs. Watts why you came to see her."

The girl whispered something Martha couldn't hear. She knelt down so she could be closer to Carlie. "I'm sorry, honey," she said. "Can you say that again?"

Carlie took a deep breath. When she spoke it sounded like, *"Doyouwanacookshhhhoolbecoseplagr."*

Martha looked up at her mother for help. Autumn laughed lightly. "She is selling cookies for her school. They need new playground equipment."

Martha smiled again at Carlie. "Of course that's what you said. I'm sorry. Sometimes my ears don't work very well."

"Probably because you're old," Carlie mumbled. Her frank expression made Martha laugh. She didn't mean any disrespect. Carlie truly believed what she'd said.

"You might be right about that," Martha said as she stood up. Her joints agreed with Carlie. "I would love to buy some cookies. Show me what kind you have."

Autumn put a large tote bag on the counter and paraded several kinds of cookies in front of Martha. After helping a customer, Mary came over and picked out a couple of boxes. Martha finally settled on two boxes of coconut macaroons and a box of fudge-striped cookies, one of Elizabeth's favorites.

While Mary paid for her order, Martha got up and walked down to the end of the counter where her purse was stashed underneath. She opened her purse and began to sort through it. It only took a few seconds for her to realize that her wallet was missing.

"Mary, my wallet isn't here," she said, trying not to panic. "Did you see anyone hanging around the counter this morning?"

Mary shook her head. "We've known everyone who's come in so far," she said. "None of them would steal from us."

Martha stood where she was and stared at her purse as if the answer were there somewhere. Then it hit her. The garage. When her purse had fallen over. "I know where it is," she said. She told Mary about spilling the contents when she'd dropped her car off.

"Can you call them and ask them to look?" Mary asked as she wrote out a check for all the cookies.

"I don't know if I can," Martha said. "And the owner made me a little uncomfortable."

"Why did you leave your car there instead of having it towed to our usual place?" Mary asked, frowning.

"It was more convenient," Martha said. "I don't want to talk about that now. I need to find my wallet. My money and my credit cards are in it."

"I hope you find your wallet," Autumn said.

"Thank you." Martha smiled at Carlie. "And I hope you sell lots of cookies."

Carlie returned Martha's smile but didn't say anything.

Autumn nudged her daughter and whispered something.

"Thank you," Carlie whispered.

"You're very welcome," Martha whispered back.

Autumn echoed Carlie's expression of gratitude. Then she took the little girl by the hand.

As mother and daughter walked out the front entrance, Mary said, "You'd better go down there yourself. Maybe it slid under the seat and no one's found it yet."

"But with Elizabeth gone..."

"I've handled the store by myself before. I can do it again. Besides, it won't take that long. Go. Really." Mary handed her keys to Martha. "Take my car."

Although Martha felt guilty about leaving Mary alone, she couldn't really do anything else. She didn't trust the garage owner with her wallet. Martha accepted the keys, grabbed her jacket and purse, and ran out to Mary's car. Then she headed for Morton's, praying her wallet was safe.

It didn't take long to get to the garage. Although the bay door was open, no one seemed to be around. After calling out for Bart, Martha got out and walked over to her car. The hood was open, which hopefully meant someone was working on it. Martha went over to the passenger's side of the car and opened the door. Praying, she slid her fingers under the seat. She felt the floor until her hand closed over something. Martha pulled it out. An empty water bottle.

She sighed. It must have fallen on the floor when she hadn't noticed. She put the bottle on the seat and tried again. This time she grasped something more promising. Her wallet! She retrieved it and then straightened up. She opened the clasp and was thrilled to find all her cash and cards still there. She put the wallet in her purse and picked up the water bottle to take it over to the large trash can near the counter. As she dropped the bottle in the trash, something caught her eye. She reached into the can and pulled out a plastic car litter bag.

Inside was an antenna topper. And not just any topper. A deer head antenna topper.

When she pulled out the topper, a piece of paper came with it, covered with coffee grounds. It looked like some kind of receipt. Cooks' Cabins was printed across the top. Martha knew about those cabins. They were located a few miles out of town, near a river that many people fished in. At one time they were only available for rental, but Martha had heard that tough times had forced the owner to sell some of them at bargain rates.

Hearing voices, Martha dropped the topper into the bag and the bag back into the can. She stuffed the receipt into her pocket. Was this the topper they'd been looking for? Was she close to finding Darlene?

"Hey, what are you doing there?"

Martha turned to see Bart standing a few yards away. His expression was far from friendly. Was he the kidnapper? Or was he in league with the person who'd taken Darlene?

"Sorry," she said with a smile. "I looked for you when I got here, but I couldn't find anyone."

Just then a door opened at the back of the garage, and a man walked through it. Martha caught a quick glance at another bay behind the one where she stood with Bart. It looked as if they were painting a car. Must be the area reserved for work like that. The man just stood near the door, glaring at her.

"I accidentally left my wallet in my car when I dropped it off," she said, trying to stay calm. "I'm just picking it up." She focused her attention on Bart. "Have you figured out what's wrong with my car?"

"I'll call you when I do," Bart said in a low voice.

Was he trying to intimidate her? Martha swallowed. She wanted to run to Mary's car, but she controlled herself. No need to make these men suspicious. Especially if they were involved with Darlene's disappearance. "Okay. Well, thanks. I'll be waiting for your call."

She turned her back and headed out of the garage, toward Mary's car. Every step she took she wondered if the men would stop her. Something was clearly going on at Morton's Auto Repair. Was it tied to Darlene? Had she been there? Martha finally reached Mary's car. She opened the door and got inside. When she looked through the windshield, she saw Bart and the other man watching her. Martha smiled, lifted her hand, and backed out of the parking lot. Neither one of the men acknowledged her gesture.

Once she was on the street, she turned the car around and headed the opposite way from Secondhand Blessings. She pulled her phone out of her purse and called Mary. She sighed when she got her sister's voice mail. "Mary, I'm so sorry to make you work alone a little longer, but I have to check something out. It's really important. I'll call you back in a little bit. I don't have time to explain, and I'm driving." She figured that her errand would be a complete waste of time anyway. Besides, she had a feeling Mary would try to talk her out of it. Maybe the name on the receipt wasn't connected to Darlene, but it was the only lead they had right now. Martha had to follow it. The waitress had been gone too long. Martha had to see if the cabins had anything to do with her disappearance.

As Martha drove, she tried to ignore the small voice in her head that kept whispering to her that she should have told Mary where she was going.

CHAPTER THIRTY-ONE

Martha drove until she reached the city limits of Lancaster and then continued on. Mary's car drove well, and the gas tank was topped off, but Martha felt uneasy when she remembered she hadn't charged her phone recently. Why hadn't she grabbed her car charger out of her car when she got her wallet? Of course, she knew the answer. She didn't think she'd need it. All she had to do was get her wallet and go home.

The woods seemed to close in on all sides, despite the sunshine filtering through the leaves. She couldn't be sure if the owner of the auto body shop was involved in some way with Darlene's disappearance, but it was possible he'd worked on the kidnapper's car. Or could it be Darlene's? No, she felt strongly that the deer head topper belonged to the kidnapper. Could Bart be in cahoots with the real estate developer? As different scenarios flashed through her mind, Martha sighed. She still wasn't sure exactly what had happened to Darlene, but one thing was certain, she wouldn't learn the truth by standing still. She thought about calling Wanda to ask her if Darlene had any connection to Cooks' Cabins, but she didn't want to use her phone. She might only have enough power for one more call, and she wanted to save it in case she needed to call her sisters.

She followed the GPS until she found the main office for Cooks' Cabins. The sign outside said the office closed at one.

She glanced at the time on the car's dashboard. It read 12:54. Just in the nick of time. She put the car into PARK and hurried up the steps. Then she pushed the front door open.

A pleasant-looking brunette woman sat behind the desk, eating a sandwich. When she saw Martha, she stuffed her meal under the desk, looking guilty. "I'm so sorry. How unprofessional of me. You caught me having a quick lunch." She waved Martha into the room. "Come in, come in. What can I help you with? Are you interested in renting one of our cabins?"

Martha shook her head as she stepped into the office. "I'm looking for a friend, but I'm not sure which cabin she might be in." The statement was true, in a way. If Darlene was being held hostage here, Martha planned to find her and bring her safely home.

"I can't disclose which cabin your friend rents, but all of our cabins are located down that road." The woman gestured out the window with a sweep of her arm.

Martha stepped farther into the room. How to ask the woman if she'd seen anyone suspicious lately without putting her on edge? "Do you mind if I ask kind of a random question?"

The woman smiled. "No problem. I've been asked all kinds of questions about our cabins. Do you know I once had a guy ask me if our cabins had dirt floors? I told him we were authentic, but not that authentic."

Martha took a deep breath. "I was wondering if you've noticed anyone new around lately. Anyone acting—out of the ordinary?"

Just like that, the woman's pleasant expression became wary. "I'm sorry. I can't give out any information about our renters." She tapped a folder on her desk. "Privacy regulations."

It had been worth a shot. Martha debated about whether or not she should venture another question, but from the woman's tight expression, it appeared she was now on the defensive.

"I understand. Thanks so much for your time." Martha left the building and climbed back into her vehicle. She headed down the road in the direction the woman had indicated. The first cabin was only a quarter of a mile from the office. Her heart pounded as she parked at the end of the driveway. If Darlene was being held against her will, it wouldn't do for Martha to announce her arrival with a spray of gravel. She walked as quietly as possible up the driveway. What was she going to say if the cabin was occupied? *Hi, I was wondering if you kidnapped a woman during the balloon festival?* What was she even looking for? She had no idea, but all their leads so far had been dead ends. The only choice now was to push forward until she had nothing left to investigate.

She knocked on the door of the first cabin. A man in a flannel shirt answered, followed by two energetic golden retrievers close on his heels and a couple of equally energetic kids. "Honey!" the man yelled over his shoulder. "Can you come help me out here? I'm trying to talk to someone at the door." A woman appeared at his side and wrestled the dogs away before ushering the children into another room.

"Sorry about that." The man stuffed his hands in his pockets. "It's a bit of a zoo around here. Can I help you?"

Martha decided to try a blunt approach. It was unlikely Darlene was being held here, with curious little kids and animals underfoot. The family didn't seem in the least suspicious.

If for some reason she was wrong though, her comment might provoke a telling reaction.

"I'm looking for my friend. Darlene O'Neal." She watched the man's face closely for a flicker of recognition, but his expression remained blank and unfazed.

He scratched his head. "No, can't say I've heard the name before. We're from out of town. Just on vacation for the weekend. Sorry."

"That's okay. Thanks for your help." Martha's heart fell as she tromped back down the driveway. She was simultaneously relieved and worried that she hadn't found Darlene. A quick drive to the second cabin proved equally futile. On her way to the third cabin, her cell phone rang from the cup holder where she'd dropped it earlier. She eased into the driveway, but by the time she'd parked, the call had already gone to voice mail. She checked the caller ID. The screen displayed the name MARY. Martha checked the voice mail message.

Hi, Martha. This is Mary. Her younger sister's voice felt familiar and welcome. *I don't know when you're getting back, but I wanted to let you know we found some more information about Darlene's disappearance. Alan Keye is in the clear. John spoke with him, and he was scouting property the night of the balloon festival. I can fill you in on more details when we talk. See you soon.*

The recording clicked off, and Martha felt her breath catch in her throat. So Alan Keye was off the hook? Who did that leave? Why was Bart acting so suspiciously? Could he be involved in some way? Nothing else made sense. But what motive would he have for kidnapping Darlene? Wanda had seemed so certain that her disappearance had been tied to something that had happened at the café, something upsetting and confidential that she had overheard. Bart had never even been mentioned as a suspect.

Martha started to dial Mary back, but her phone died just as she began to place the call. She mentally kicked herself again for not taking the time to make sure her phone was charged this morning. Now she was in a vulnerable spot with no way to contact anyone.

She knew she should probably head back to Secondhand Blessings and meet up with her sisters while they figured out a new course of action, but she couldn't shake the feeling that Darlene was close. She would finish investigating the cabins, then she'd head back to Bird-in-Hand. Besides, if Bart was the kidnapper, he was still back at the garage. He'd been working on a car as she left, and she was certain no one had followed her as she drove here.

Her decision made, she got out of her vehicle. As she made her way toward the cabin, she couldn't shake the sensation that she was being watched. She dismissed the feeling. How silly. She was just jumpy after Mary's phone call. She'd seen no one on the road behind her, and she'd watched carefully. She was alone out here—unless, of course, Darlene was in the cabin directly ahead of her. The thought propelled her forward.

Though the main office for Cooks' Cabins had looked neat and well maintained, this cabin appeared neglected. Run-down. The grass was overgrown, and the front porch was cluttered with random objects—gas cans, broken boards, an old lawn mower, an armchair sprouting a layer of mold.

Little matter if Darlene was inside. Martha started for the porch when something on the ground caught her eye. She bent down to retrieve part of a broken nametag. She turned it over to see Two-Bi and under that DARL printed on the fragment. The rest was missing. A chill coursed down her spine, and the hair on her arms stood up. She'd found Darlene.

She turned, planning to run to the car and drive back to the office. She could use their phone to call the police. Before she had a chance to move she heard a noise behind her, and she felt a sharp pain in her head. Suddenly the world was dark.

CHAPTER THIRTY-TWO

W here's Martha?" Elizabeth had finished up helping out at Rachel's variety stand and had just made it back to Secondhand Blessings for the afternoon shift.

Mary patted a stool behind the counter and motioned for Elizabeth to sit. "Martha went to Morton's. She thinks she dropped her wallet there the other day." Mary pinched the top of her nose with her fingers. "If she doesn't find it there, I'd almost be inclined to think it's been stolen."

"Stolen? Why do you say that?" Elizabeth asked.

Mary looked embarrassed. "Oh, I guess I'm just talking out loud. Thinking of John's warnings about Arnold."

Elizabeth hated that Arnold would be under suspicion. He hadn't shown up at the variety stand again. She wasn't sure whether she felt relieved or disappointed. John might be right— the guy might be bad news all around, but she couldn't help feeling sympathy for him. There was always hope for people, as long as they had breath in them.

Mary checked her cell phone, which was sitting on the front counter. "Oh. There's a missed call from Martha. She must have phoned when I was busy checking a customer out a few minutes ago. I didn't see it."

"Did she leave a voice mail?" asked Elizabeth.

Mary checked. "She did. Let me find out why she called." She pressed the phone to her ear and listened to the message. Then she punched a button and set the phone back down on the counter. A worried look crossed her face. "I guess she's already been to Morton's. She didn't say if she'd found her wallet or not. Just that she had to 'check something out,' whatever that means, and that she'd call back soon."

Elizabeth felt a small flicker of uneasiness. "Do you think she had an errand to run?"

"I don't know. She didn't say much. It didn't quite sound like that though. I wonder—" Mary stopped talking and drummed her fingers on the countertop absently.

"What?"

Mary paused. "You don't think she found something out about Darlene, do you? That she's going off on her own to investigate?"

"I wouldn't think so." Martha was normally so pragmatic. Elizabeth had to admit though, her sister had definitely had an impatient streak lately that had clouded her judgment on more than one occasion. Was it possible Martha had found something and was tracking Darlene's kidnapper on her own?

"Maybe we should look for her," Mary said, starting to rise from her seat.

Elizabeth sighed. Martha hated to be babied. If she really was just running errands, how foolish would she feel if her sisters made a big deal out of her being gone a few extra minutes? Elizabeth shrugged off her concerns. "She has her cell phone with her. She said she'd call you back soon. Maybe we should wait a little bit longer."

"All right," said Mary, settling back into her chair with visible reluctance.

The sisters worked for another hour, checking out a steady stream of customers. All the while, Mary kept an eagle eye trained on her phone, though no calls came through. "Shouldn't we have heard from her by now?" Mary asked Elizabeth when the store was empty again.

Elizabeth still wasn't overly worried, but she wasn't totally at peace either. "Why don't you try her phone again? See if she answers?" she suggested.

Mary found Martha's number and held the phone to her ear. Within a few seconds, she shook her head. "It went straight to voice mail. Lizzie, I think something's wrong. I don't know why, but I just feel uneasy."

"I do too," Elizabeth admitted. "I'm sure she's fine, but maybe we could run by Morton's and make sure she found her wallet. Bart or whoever's working today might have an idea where she went."

The sisters closed the shop before heading to Morton's in Elizabeth's SUV. When they arrived, no one was at the front desk. Someone was obviously working though. Elizabeth could hear a lot of hisses and pops of machinery. "Hello?" she called into the open shop. "Anyone here?"

"Hold on." A gruff voice answered her from a back area of the garage. "I'll be right there." The noises stopped, and Bart appeared from a tarped-off space, his clothes splattered with paint. A gleam of recognition dawned on his face when he saw Elizabeth. "What do you want?"

Elizabeth was a bit taken aback by his blunt greeting. "I was here the other day with my sister, Martha. Do you remember me?"

"I remember you." Bart's tone wasn't hostile, but it certainly wasn't welcoming either.

"Has Martha been here today? She thought she lost something in her car."

"She came by around lunchtime," Bart said slowly. Again, the words seemed civil enough, but Elizabeth thought she detected an underlying note of tension running under them.

"We're trying to get in touch with her," Mary said. "I wonder if you'd let us look in her car to make sure she got what she needed." She made her voice extra sweet. Elizabeth couldn't help but think it was a smart move. *A gentle answer turns away wrath.* But would it work on Bart?

His face was stony. Apparently not. "Listen, I didn't give your sister—whatever her name is—grief about sneaking back there, because it's her car, but I'm sure not going to let you."

Mary started to protest. "We only want to see if—"

Bart slapped his hand down on the counter with enough force that the sound echoed through the garage. "I'm tired of people snooping around, acting like they have the run of the place! This is *my* business, do you understand?" He leaned forward on the counter in an aggressive stance that told Elizabeth they needed to back off.

"We're sorry for bothering you," she said quickly, taking Mary's arm and pulling her out to the parking lot.

"Why did you do that?" Mary asked once they were inside Elizabeth's vehicle. "Don't you think he acted a little suspiciously? Why would someone get so angry over a simple question?"

"I'm not sure." Elizabeth dug in her purse for her cell phone. "I don't think it would be a bad idea to call John and see what he thinks." She punched in the number and had a brief conversation with John, who said he was in the area and insisted on stopping by the shop to talk with Bart.

Waiting for him to arrive, Elizabeth and Mary took turns dialing Martha's cell phone, but it continued going directly to voice mail. "I'm really worried," Mary said. Elizabeth noticed that her voice shook.

"I know you're concerned," Elizabeth said. "But we're doing everything we can right now except for the most important thing. Why don't we pray?" God knew Martha's location and Darlene's too, for that matter. He had created them, and He cared for the two women even more than their relatives could.

Mary sighed, and her shoulders relaxed. "That would be good."

As they were finishing their prayer, John arrived, and the three of them walked back into Morton's. Bart leveled a glare when he saw Elizabeth and Mary reenter the shop, trailed by a police officer. "Is there a problem, Officer?" he asked John.

"The ladies said you got a little snippy with them," John said.

Bart raised his chin in a gesture of defiance, even though Elizabeth noticed he was a good few inches shorter than John. "They were being nosy. Wanting free run of my shop.

I've got heavy equipment back there. This is a business, not a playground."

Elizabeth bristled at the condescending remark.

John raised his eyebrows. "I'm assuming you won't mind if I take a look around?"

Bart glared at John, who casually reached for his radio. Bart's face paled, and he rushed to speak. He was obviously more bark than bite. "N–no...sir."

"Good." John smiled. "That's what I thought. Now, can you show me around the place?"

"H–happy to." Bart led John into the recesses of the shop. As they left, Mary immediately pulled out her cell phone and tried to dial Martha again.

"Still going to voice mail?" Elizabeth asked as Mary put her phone back into her purse.

Mary clutched her purse in front of her, looking miserable. "Where could she be, Lizzie? Where's Martha?"

CHAPTER THIRTY-THREE

When Martha woke up, she tried to reach up and touch her head. It hurt. But she couldn't move her hands. They were tied behind her. She realized she was sitting in a chair and that her ankles were bound as well. She peered through the murky darkness, her nose twitching at an almost overwhelming mustiness. Where was she?

"Martha Watts?"

Martha jumped at the sound of a woman's voice. "Yes?"

Her eyes were beginning to adjust to the dim lighting. She could see someone sitting in a chair several yards away from her.

"It's Darlene O'Neal. From the Two Bird Café?"

Tears sprang to Martha's eyes. "Darlene? We've been looking everywhere for you. Are you all right?"

"Yes. But I don't know how much longer that will be true. We could both be in real danger."

"What do you mean?"

"When he leaves, I'm not sure he'll want us around to tell people what he did."

Martha took a deep breath, trying to calm herself and ignore the pounding in her head. She must have been hit on the head. "He? Who did this, Darlene? The night of the balloon festival I tried to see who abducted you, but it was just too dark. My sisters and I have been doing everything we can to find you."

"Is someone coming? Will they get us out of here?"

Martha's heart sank as she realized how foolish she had been. In her haste to locate Darlene, she'd made stupid mistakes. She should have taken the time to tell Mary where she was going and about Bart's strange manner at the garage. And she shouldn't have taken off for the cabins with a phone that wasn't charged. How could she have been so reckless?

"I...I don't know if anyone's coming, Darlene. I didn't tell my sisters I was headed here. It was a silly thing to do. I'm so sorry."

Darlene's sob tore at Martha. "Tell me who brought you here, Darlene," she said, trying to keep her voice calm and steady. This wasn't the time to lose their heads. "Wanda told us you overheard something at the café the night you disappeared. Something that may have led to the kidnapping. But we've followed every lead. Talked to everyone who acted suspiciously that night. All the roads led to...nothing."

"I did overhear something," Darlene answered.

By now, Martha's vision had adjusted even more to the dim light. She could clearly see Darlene. She appeared to be in good health. Relief washed over Martha. As she gazed around the room she saw a bed against one wall.

"What was it?" Martha asked. "Who took you?"

Suddenly light flooded the room. For the first time Martha was able to see around her. She understood the mustiness now. They were in a cellar.

Martha squinted up toward the cellar door that had been pulled open. A figure stood there, but she couldn't make out who it was because of the way the light came from behind him.

"Answer her, Darlene," a gruff male voice barked out.

Darlene began to cry again, and Martha realized she wasn't able to respond to the kidnapper's orders. "Why don't *you* tell me," Martha said forcefully.

The man laughed and walked down the stairs until Martha was able to see him. She gasped when she realized who was standing at the bottom step, glaring at her. Thoughts began flitting through her brain like frightened butterflies.

"No one called to say Darlene was going to visit her sister, did they?" Martha asked. "We thought the kidnapper forced Darlene to make that call. But you lied. Why didn't we see it?"

"Because it never occurred to you that my boss would do something like this to me," Darlene sputtered.

Hal Bailey stepped down onto the dirt floor of the cellar. "I really thought she had a sister," he said. "I was convinced you'd figure out I was the one who—"

"Abducted Darlene?" Martha finished for him.

Hal shrugged. "I like to say *temporarily detained*, but that's up to you."

"But why? What did she overhear that you didn't want her to tell anyone?"

Hal sat down on the steps. "I guess I owe you an explanation before I leave."

"You're leaving?" Martha asked. "What about us?"

"Cool your jets. I'll explain everything—but it will be the condensed version. I have a plane to catch."

Martha started to ask another question, but he silenced her by putting his finger to his lips. "You need to shut up if you want to hear the truth."

Although questions kept popping into her mind, Martha clamped her lips together.

It seemed that Hal took this as a sign for him to continue. The truth was, Martha was trying to figure out how to stall. Although she hadn't told Mary where she was going, she hoped somehow she and Elizabeth would figure it out. Maybe they'd called John and were questioning Bart right now. If he was involved and knew where Darlene was, maybe he'd tell them. She wanted to keep Hal engaged and talking as long as possible. Not just so he'd be caught, but also so he wouldn't decide to shut them up for good.

Hal heaved a deep sigh. "On certain nights, after the café closed, I invited select people into the large storage building behind the restaurant. Let's just say I offered some *games* for people to play. I needed the money. I don't clear enough from the café to live the kind of lifestyle I want to be accustomed to." He laughed as if he'd said something funny.

"Games?" Martha echoed, confused.

"Gambling," Darlene said quietly.

Martha remembered Arnold. The first time she'd seen him was in back of the Two Bird Café. So that was why he was down on his luck. Gambling.

"And you overheard something about that?" she asked, looking at Darlene.

"Hal didn't know I was in the kitchen when he talked to one of the bookies he works with."

"When she tried to run out, I knew she'd heard me taking a bet over the phone."

"So what? I mean, it's not legal, but it's not that bad, is it?" Martha asked. "To go through all this. To kidnap Darlene—"

"You don't understand," Hal snarled. "I've been saving up money for a while. At first I thought I'd use it to keep the café going. But then I realized I could take in a great deal of money...and leave this stupid town." He smiled. "I'm headed to a country with no extradition policy. A place where I can live, really live, for the first time in my life."

"That would take a great deal of money," Martha said, frowning. "How much could you have possibly made from a small-town gambling enterprise?"

"He's planning to take off with other people's money," Darlene said. "Without paying them their winnings."

"Thank you, Darlene," Hal said with disdain. "I can speak for myself."

"But don't you have to pay gamblers at the time they win?" Martha shook her head. "This doesn't make any sense."

Hal laughed, a deep rumbling sound, but there wasn't any joy in it. "'Tis the season to bet on who'll be in the play-offs and eventually the World Series. I stumbled onto some sports gamblers with deep pockets. Since I'd always paid my debts, they were willing to plunk down a great deal of money before the games were played. But unfortunately for them, I won't be around to pay their winnings, which are quite substantial."

Martha wondered if Hal had put himself in the crosshairs of some people who could be very dangerous. But at the moment she didn't care about that. She just wanted to make sure she and Darlene made it out of this alive.

"So you kidnapped Darlene to keep her quiet?" Martha asked. "Wasn't there another way to go about it?"

Hal shrugged. "I didn't know what else to do. I couldn't allow her to contact the police. Not when I was so close to finally getting out of here. I left the café and waited in Greer's parking lot. Darlene's schedule never changes. Always leaves at the same time. Always takes the same route home. When I figured she was close, I called her cell phone and told her my car had run out of gas. I asked her for help."

"And like an idiot, I pulled into the parking lot where he said he was stranded," Darlene said, her voice trembling. "Even though I realized he was running a gambling business, I never thought he'd do something like this. I should have been more suspicious."

Martha thought Hal looked as though he felt guilty for a moment, but it didn't last long. "I did what I had to do," he said in a low voice.

Martha sighed. "And then our balloon drifted overhead."

"I was praying you'd see me," Darlene said. "And get help."

"We did," Martha said. "But by the time the police reached the parking lot the car was gone."

"My car is behind the cabin, covered with a tarp," Darlene said.

"And my car is at Morton's Garage, being repainted and sold." Hal glared at Martha. "I had no idea if you'd seen it, but I couldn't take the chance. I've been driving my brother's truck." He pointed upwards. "This cabin was his. He died a few months ago. I miss him, but having access to this place and to his truck saved me." He frowned at her. "How did you find me?"

Martha hesitated. She had no intention of mentioning the charms. She wasn't sure how Hal would react to that news. "Your car antenna topper. We saw it on video taken from a drone flying over the festival. When I was at Morton's garage, I saw one in the trash with a receipt for this cabin. I wasn't certain the topper was the one we saw. I was just trying to follow anything that could lead me to Darlene."

Hal's sharp intake of breath made it clear he was surprised. "My brother bought that topper right before he died and gave it to me because we enjoyed hunting together. That's the only reason I had it on my car. I wasn't planning on throwing it away. Bart should have asked me before he tossed it out."

"I don't understand something," Martha said. "How could you move two cars from the parking lot so quickly?" Before Hal responded, Martha had already figured out the answer. "Bart. You used Bart at Morton's to help you."

Hal's eyes narrowed. "You're pretty smart. He and his son met me at Greer's. Bart drove my car to his shop and his son drove their truck back home. I brought Darlene's car here."

I'm obviously not smart enough, or the police would be on their way here now.

He stood. "It's time to say goodbye, ladies. I have a life to live. No more slinging hash and listening to customers complain about their food."

"What...what are you going to do with us?" Darlene asked. Exactly what Martha was wondering.

Hal's eyes widened. "Surely you don't think..." He shook his head. "I may be a gambler, but I'm not a killer, Darlene. Too bad you don't know that."

"You kidnapped two people," Martha said, trying to keep him from leaving. "That's not the kind of person that inspires trust."

"Point taken." He sighed. "Once I'm far enough away, I'll call the police on a burner phone and tell them you're here."

Martha grunted. "And how long will it take you to get 'far enough away'?"

"Not a problem he needs to worry about," a voice said.

Martha almost cried when she looked up to see John standing at the top of the stairs, his gun trained on Hal.

CHAPTER THIRTY-FOUR

Martha stood in front of the cabin with her sisters and Darlene. They watched as John put Hal in the back of the patrol car. Then John walked over to where they waited.

"I need all of you to come down to the station so I can take statements." He nodded toward Darlene. "You've been held for over a week in that cellar. I think it would be best if you went to the hospital so they can check you out. I'll get your statement later."

She shook her head. "Hal took good care of me. Made sure I had whatever I needed. Brought me food and let me go upstairs to use the bathroom. I'm fine, really."

Martha put her hand on Darlene's arm. "I agree with John," she said. "You really should get checked out. Just in case."

"That goes for you too, Martha," John said. "You were struck on the head, and you need to be seen by a doctor."

Martha shook her head. "I'm okay, but if it makes everyone feel better I'll call my own doctor on Monday."

Darlene smiled. "I'll go, but I want to give a statement first. Then I'll visit the hospital. Okay?"

"All right. I guess I can live with that," John said.

"What about my car?" Darlene asked him.

"It will have to stay where it is for now. I'm afraid it's evidence. We'll get it back to you as soon as we can."

Darlene sighed. "Okay. I understand." She shook her head. "No car. No job. Boy, this is going to be a challenge."

"You'll get a new job," Elizabeth said. "Someone will hire you."

"I hope so," Darlene said. "I sure will miss the Two Bird though. I like that little diner."

"We do too," Mary said. "But the most important thing is that you're okay."

Darlene's eyes filled with tears as she gazed at the sisters. "Thank you all so much. If it hadn't been for you…"

"Well, it seems that Hal would have made sure you were rescued after he left town," Martha said.

"He says he was going to call someone," Darlene said, her voice shaky with emotion. "But what if he was lying? Leaving us there would have made sure he was safe for a while. He could have easily taken the easy way out. We could have died, tied to those chairs."

Martha still felt that Hal would have notified someone about them, but Darlene was right. What if he'd changed his mind?

"Martha just wouldn't quit," Elizabeth said. "She was bound and determined to find you."

"Thank you, Martha," Darlene said, her voice choked with emotion.

Martha nodded at her, too moved to speak.

They followed John to the police station. Once they arrived, they were led to a small conference room.

"So the antenna topper led you to the cabins?" Darlene asked once they were seated.

"The charm from your bracelet put us on the right trail," Martha said. "I don't know if we would have found you without that. The topper wasn't a very strong clue at first. The high school glee club had just sold them for a fundraiser. But only people who went to Camp Hollyoaks had those charms. It helped us narrow down the list of people who could have been abducted."

Darlene laughed softly. "The charm must have come off when Hal grabbed me. The hook that held the charm to my bracelet had been loose for a while. I'd been meaning to get it fixed for some time now, but now I'm so glad I didn't."

"Then I found part of your diner nametag in the dirt on the driveway of the cabin," Martha said.

"I fought with Hal again when we got here," Darlene told her. "It must have fallen off my uniform, and one of us must have stepped on it."

"That, along with the topper, convinced me I'd found you," said Martha. "Unfortunately, Hal saw me. After that, it was all up to my sisters and John. Bart told them about Hal's call the night he took you. He didn't want to get in trouble with the police."

"Well, if he knew Hal was kidnapping Darlene, he's going to be charged as an accomplice, isn't he?" Elizabeth asked.

"I would think so," said Martha.

"Seems like God's hand was in this all along," Mary said. "If that charm hadn't fallen off in the parking lot, and if Martha hadn't found that nametag in front of the cabin…"

"I agree," Darlene said, wiping away a tear that fell down her cheek. "I prayed so hard that someone would find me. As time went on, I have to admit, I was beginning to lose hope."

"I'm sorry it took us so long," Martha said.

"Don't be," Darlene said with a smile. "God got you there right in time."

"I have a bone to pick with you," Elizabeth said, her gaze focused on Martha. "You should have told us you were going to the cabins. We had no idea where you were. We were so worried."

"I'm sorry," Martha said, "but I'd forgotten to charge my phone and was almost out of power. Besides, I wasn't sure going to the cabins would result in anything helpful. I planned to just look around, and if I saw anything suspicious, I'd call John." She sighed. "Of course, having a dead phone made even that impossible."

"You're usually very well organized," Mary said. "You always make sure your phone is charged, and you take your car in to be serviced regularly. This last week you've been so impulsive."

"I know. You're right." Martha shook her head. "I was just so afraid something would happen to Darlene, and it would be my fault." She looked at Darlene with tears in her eyes. "I believed you saw us in that balloon, and you were counting on us—on me—to save you."

Darlene reached over and gave Martha a quick hug. "I was," she said. "And you did."

"But it took us so long—"

Darlene stepped back and held up her hand. "Stop saying that. Please. What you did was wonderful. Above and beyond what most people would ever do." She smiled at Martha. "Promise me you'll quit feeling guilty. I will forever appreciate your efforts. Okay?"

Martha summoned a smile. "Okay. I promise. I'll just be happy you're free."

The door to the small room opened, and John stepped inside. "Well, he's booked. And singing like a bird." John walked over to the table. "I think his brother's death really affected Hal. He wanted to leave town and start a new life. Felt like there were too many reminders of his brother here. He came up with the idea of skipping town with money that didn't belong to him and got carried away." He shrugged. "It doesn't excuse what he did, but I thought you might want to know the reason behind his...bad choices."

"I want to feel sorry for him, but I can't yet," Darlene said. "I was so scared. Eventually, I realized he wasn't going to hurt me, but at first I wasn't sure."

"I understand," John said. "I'll bring some statement forms in a minute and have you fill them out. But first, you have a visitor." John went back out into the hallway and pushed a wheelchair into the room.

"Daddy!" Darlene said. She got up and put her arms around her father.

Clyde reached up and patted his daughter's back. "I'm so sorry," he said. "I thought you'd gone away on purpose. You've done that before...."

Darlene took a step back and stared at her father. "Dad, I haven't gone anywhere without telling you since I was a teenager."

"I...I guess that's right," Clyde said. "I should have realized you were in trouble."

"It doesn't matter now," Darlene said. "These ladies found me, and I'm safe now. And I promise I'll always make sure you know where I am from here on out."

"That sounds great," Clyde said. His gaze swung to Martha and her sisters. "I'll never be able to thank you enough for finding my daughter."

"We're just happy she's safe," Martha said.

"Clyde's going to wait out here until you're done, Darlene," John said.

"I'll be out there soon, Daddy."

"Then you're going to the hospital, right?" Martha asked.

Darlene sighed. "Yes. I really just want to go home and sleep. But if it will make you feel better…"

"It will," Martha said.

"I'm going to need transportation," Darlene said slowly.

"I'll take you," John said. "And I'll make sure you and your father get home."

Martha wanted to offer to take Darlene to the hospital, but she was exhausted. Now that Darlene was safe, she was so relieved that the tension from the past week that had kept her going had evaporated.

"We need to celebrate Darlene's homecoming," Mary said. "How about we all meet for lunch tomorrow after church?"

"That sounds great," Martha said. "We'll come by and get you…and your father."

"Thanks, but I can drive my father's car. I appreciate the offer though."

Martha smiled. Her heart was full of thanksgiving to God for helping them find Darlene.

CHAPTER THIRTY-FIVE

Martha thought she would be exhausted the next morning, given the ordeal she'd been through. But she woke bright and early on Sunday. She felt as if a burden had been lifted from her. She got dressed quickly, and she and her sisters headed to the early service at Mount Zion Mennonite Church. Martha felt herself tearing up as they sang the words to the first hymn, "His Eye Is on the Sparrow."

Why should I feel discouraged?
Why should the shadows come?

What an apt description of how she'd been feeling lately. Bearing the entire weight of finding Darlene and solving the mystery of her disappearance on her own. Impatient because she thought it was all up to her, and if she did things less than perfectly, the situation would have a bad outcome.

Though by the path He leadeth
But one step I may see...

But God had been there the entire time. He knew the beginning from the end, and He had everything in His hands. He saw the big picture, the Bird's Eye View. The thought comforted Martha. It wasn't all up to her to fix everything. She smiled as she listened to the sweet harmonies of the congregation weaving together.

His eye is on the sparrow,

And I know He watches me.

Martha wiped some moisture from her eyes and glanced over at Elizabeth to see if she shared her emotions, but to her surprise, Elizabeth had a frown on her face. The song ended, and her older sister glanced down at the empty seat beside her, then sighed and clasped her hands in front of her. Who was she expecting?

"Excuse me, is this seat taken?" A man asked the question, and Martha watched as a lovely smile slowly lit up Elizabeth's face. John Marks stood next to her, wearing a navy suit and tie and looking embarrassed. "I'm sorry I'm late."

Elizabeth shook her head. "You're fine." She took his arm and pulled him into the pew. "I'm so glad you could come." Her response was low-key, but Martha noticed that her sister was grinning like a Cheshire cat as she sank into her seat.

The music done, Pastor Nagle strode up to the pulpit. A burly man, he looked like the last person to wax poetic on scripture, but he routinely turned out eloquent sermons. It had been tough to transition to a new pastor after Pastor Zook left, but Pastor Nagle led the church well.

Pastor Nagle cleared his throat. "What a fitting song to lead into today's sermon. 'His eye is on the sparrow, and I know He watches me.'" He directed the congregation to open their Bibles, and he spent the next hour expounding on how God watched carefully over His children. Thinking of her own children—Craig, Trish, and Kyle—caused more tears to pool in Martha's eyes. All those memories she and Chuck had shared together. The ache of missing her husband had lessened over time, but Chuck would always be the only man for her. She thought of Lillian and the music box they were fixing for her at Comstock Jeweler's. Tomorrow, Martha would call and check on it. It helped ease the ache in her heart even more to think that she could comfort another widow in her grief.

After the offertory and altar call, the service drew to a close. "Do you think that's really true?" John asked, as they stood to leave the sanctuary.

"Is what really true?" Elizabeth filed out of the row after him.

"What the pastor said, about God taking care of us."

"The Bible says God made people in His own image," Elizabeth said. "Even though He's perfect, without sin, and we make mistakes all the time, He knows what we're like. And He wants connection with us. Relationship. It's the entire story of the Bible, how Jesus came to earth as a sacrifice for our sins so our broken relationship with God could be restored."

"I'm beginning to see that," John said slowly.

"You know, the church hosts a Bible study every Wednesday night."

"It's casual," Mary added, glancing at John's suit. "You can even wear jeans."

"You should stop by if you're not working," Elizabeth said. "It's a good place to ask questions, and Pastor Nagle is really easy to talk to."

John smiled. "I might just do that."

Elizabeth's eyes shone. "We can talk about it at lunch if you want."

"I'd like that very much," John said. "That is, if your sisters are okay with me tagging along."

Mary grinned. "No complaint from me."

"The more the merrier," Martha said with a smile. "Let's get going. I'm starving." She was pleased to see Elizabeth so happy, and John really did seem sincere in his interest. As they left the sanctuary, they passed by early arrivals to the more traditional service that would be taking place in about half an hour. Martha smiled at several of the people she recognized, until a familiar face stopped her cold. "Arnold!"

The man was nearly unrecognizable, wearing a nice sweater and sport coat instead of his usual threadbare clothing. His hair was neatly combed into place, and he'd shaved off the dark stubble that had covered his face before. He stood in the space awkwardly, as though he wasn't sure where to go.

Elizabeth hurried over to him. "Arnold! I'm so happy you could make it. I see the sport coat fits you well." Martha looked closer at the man's clothing and realized Elizabeth must have gifted him some of their secondhand wares. Elizabeth's kindness made Martha temper her own hesitance, and she and Mary both greeted Arnold. Even John, normally so on guard with the man, shook hands with him.

"I hate for you to sit in the service alone," Elizabeth said. "If you had come to the early service, you would have been more than welcome to sit with us."

Arnold waved off her concern. "It's okay. I'm actually supposed to meet my daughter here. She recently moved back to the area, and we've reconnected." He looked down toward his feet, then up again at their group. "I've not been proud of the choices I've made the last couple of years. I think it's time to turn over a new leaf and do things the right way."

"That's a wonderful decision." Martha smiled at Arnold. "And church is a great way to start your journey."

Martha wasn't sure how things would go with Arnold. With Hal in custody, would Arnold also have legal problems? John had hinted that they might ask Arnold to testify about the ring. It was possible that if he helped the authorities, he might avoid prison. She hoped so, but whatever happened, with God in his life, Arnold would be much happier.

Jennie's, also known as the Route 30 Diner, was packed when John and the sisters arrived for lunch. The décor could best be described as "vintage," since the owner hadn't changed its look for many years. Martha smiled. She had many fond memories of coming here as a child, sitting on red pleather stools at the chrome-edged counter opposite the booth they sat in now. They had just ordered their drinks when Darlene, pushing Clyde in his wheelchair, showed up to join them.

"Darlene!" Martha jumped to her feet and threw her arms around her. "I'm so glad you could meet us. How are you feeling?"

Darlene smiled. "Just fine. It feels so good to get out of that cellar."

"And one thing's for sure," John said. "Hal isn't going to be bothering anybody else for a long time."

"That's a relief," Darlene said.

"Do you know what you're going to do now?" Elizabeth asked. "If you'd like to help us out at our store temporarily, we would be happy to pay you to sort inventory."

"Oh, no, no." Darlene shook her head emphatically. "I couldn't ask more of you than you've already given me. Besides"— she laid her hand on her father's shoulder—"I have some things to keep me busy for a while."

"Oh? What's that?"

Darlene had a tender look in her eye as she locked gazes with her father. "I'm going to move back home for a while and help Dad out. I haven't spent as much time with him as I should. And I certainly won't miss that dingy old apartment I was renting."

"I forgot how much I missed having my Dee around." Clyde's eyes misted over, though he made a big show of acting as though he had something in his eye. "Besides, it'll be nice to have her there to help me with all the things I've fallen behind on since my accident."

"If only I was handier with tools," Darlene joked.

"Actually, I may be able to help you with that…," Martha said slowly. She remembered seeing Jim Conner at church that morning. "I have a friend, Jim, who owns a house restoration company. I'm sure he'd be able to help you with any repair work or maintenance you need done at your home. Would it be all right if I gave him your number?"

"That would be just great," Darlene said. "Oh, thank you again."

John, who had been quietly listening, said, "You know, I don't know if this is something you'd be interested in, Darlene, but I heard the Two Bird might not be closing its doors like we all thought."

"No?" Darlene looked surprised.

John shook his head. "Seems Alan Keye has expressed an interest in buying the property, and he might keep the diner going. It'll take a while to get all the paperwork taken care of, but I think he'll be looking for some good people to help him."

"I thought Alan Keye was a real estate agent," Martha said. "What's he doing buying the diner? Doesn't he specialize in residential properties?"

"Well, he's also a developer," John replied.

Darlene pursed her lips. "Thanks so much for thinking of me, but I'm not sure if I want to get back into waitressing again. It's too hard on the joints, and let's face it—" She laughed, a full, throaty sound. "I'm not getting any younger."

John shook his head. "You misunderstood me. I didn't mean you should work as a waitress. I think you might approach Alan about working as management."

Darlene's eyes grew wide. "Me? Run a restaurant?" She laughed. "All I have is a high school diploma. Not a fancy business degree."

"I know a lot of self-made entrepreneurs who didn't go the college route. Your father is one of them." John smiled at Clyde, whose own lips quirked into a grin. Darlene didn't say much as the rest of them talked, but Martha could tell the wheels were turning in her brain.

As the conversation turned to another topic, Mary picked up her menu and began scanning the lunch options. "Ooh, the club sandwich sounds good. What are you going to have, Lizzie?"

Elizabeth squinted at the list and pursed her lips. "I'm not sure. Maybe a burger."

"I wonder where our waitress is." Clyde searched the restaurant, tapping his fingers on the tabletop. "I'm starving."

Martha just smiled and leaned back into the cushioning of the booth as everyone chatted about their food choices. She'd certainly learned her lesson. No more hurried gestures from her. At least not today. No, right now, she was perfectly content to sit patiently right here, with her favorite people, savoring the feeling that everything—at least for this sweet, present moment—was right with the world.

A NOTE FROM THE AUTHORS

Dear Reader,

Have you ever been caught in a season of life where things felt out of control? I know I have, and I imagine most people can relate. Martha feels precisely this way in *Bird's Eye View*. She's the Classen sister most used to taking control and becomes frustrated when the twisting mystery she and her sisters are attempting to solve grows progressively more confusing. She reacts with impatience, trying to force the situation to unfold on her timeline.

How much easier and more pleasant would the journey be if we were better at discerning when we need to push a matter—and when we need to release control to God? He's the one who always has a bird's-eye view of events, and He's the one we can always rely on in our time of greatest need. I pray this story encourages you. Thanks so much for reading!

Blessings!
Shaen

Dear Reader,

I've really enjoyed writing about the Classen sisters! And one of the nicest aspects of this journey was writing with my daughter-in-law. Since this is my last book in this series, I want to thank Shaen for sharing her gifts with me. It thrills me to see her step into her destiny, and I want her to know how proud I am of her.

I think everyone who reads about Elizabeth, Martha, and Mary will identify with them in some way. As Shaen mentioned, we may see our impatience expressed in Martha, but we should also applaud her compassion. Elizabeth's sense of family endears her to all of us. Although Mary's enthusiasm occasionally gets her into trouble, she has a heart of gold. The way all three sisters work together regardless of their differences is such an example for all of us. When we value our dissimilarities, we're stronger. The sisters are a great example of the kind of unity we should all strive for.

I think you'll enjoy this story. Thank you for allowing us to be a part of your lives.

God bless you,
Nancy

ABOUT THE AUTHORS

Shaen Layle

Shaen Layle is a *USA Today* bestselling author who writes inspirational cozy mysteries from her home in the Midwest, where she lives with her artist husband and two rambunctious but adorable little boys. Trained as a literary novelist and with a decade of librarianship under her belt, she loves discussing all things bookish with her readers on social media and on her website at shaenlayle.com. You can sign up for her newsletter to receive exclusive content and sneak peeks of future books at shaenlayle.com/newsletter.

Nancy Mehl

Nancy Mehl is a *USA Today* bestselling author. She's written almost forty books and has been a finalist for the Carol Award twice and won the award once. She was also a finalist for two Reviewers' Choice Awards from RT Book Reviews and was a finalist for the coveted Christy Award. She lives in Missouri with her husband, Norman, and her puggle, Watson.

Readers can learn more about Nancy through her website: nancymehl.com. She is part of the Suspense Sisters: suspense-sisters.blogspot.com along with several other popular suspense authors. She is also very active on Facebook.

MORE TO THE STORY

A Bird's-Eye View of Bird-in-Hand

I (Shaen) have been blessed to partake of many adventures in my life with some dear friends who are more like sisters. Together, we've white-water rafted the Ocoee River, ridden horseback through the Great Smoky Mountain National Forest, and even hiked a biblical aqueduct in Israel in pitch-black darkness with water up to our waists! Still, one thing on my bucket list that I haven't gotten around to accomplishing yet is the adventure Martha goes on with her sisters: riding in a hot-air balloon.

Each September, Lancaster County holds its annual weekend-long Hot-Air Balloon Festival. On the ground, participants are kept happy with s'mores, food trucks, and tethered balloon rides for kids and adults. In-air events take place during the day, such as the popular Hound & Hare Race where practiced balloon teams "chase" each other to a finish line, and continue into the night, with the incandescent Nighttime Balloon Glow. You can also book private or shared balloon rides—just like Martha, Mary, and Elizabeth—to get an aerial view of the fall splendor Amish Country has to offer, an adventure not to be missed if you're ever given the opportunity.

FRESH FROM MARTHA'S KITCHEN

Tears on My Pillow Pie

Ingredients:

⅓ cup butter, melted

1½ cups brown sugar, packed

2 eggs

1 tablespoon flour

½ cup evaporated milk

1 unbaked 9" pie crust

Instructions:

Preheat oven to 350 F.

Combine butter, brown sugar, eggs, flour, and milk. Mix well.

Pour into pie crust.

Bake for 15 minutes or until crust is light brown.

Turn off heat and leave pie in the oven for 1 hour or until set.

Read on for a sneak peek of another exciting book
in the Mysteries of Lancaster County series!

Dairy Disaster
by Elizabeth Ludwig

A buzz filled Secondhand Blessings. It bounced from the ceiling stretching high overhead and settled in the nooks between shelves. It was a mixture of excitement and energy and…anticipation? Yes, that was it.

Elizabeth smiled as she took a sip of her pumpkin spice–flavored coffee. October was always filled with anticipation, like the whole world knew change was coming and held its breath while it waited for the leaves to signal the season.

"*Guten morgen,* everyone." Rachel Fischer's clear voice quieted the women of the quilting circle who met at Secondhand Blessings every Thursday morning. Clad in a plain blue dress with a white prayer *kapp* holding her chocolate-brown hair firmly in place, she made a sweet picture framed against the barn's painted wall. She extended her hand toward the ring of chairs set up around a wide table at the center of the store. "If you would take your seats?"

Empty cup in hand, Elizabeth turned away to begin the day's tasks. She attended the quilting circle on occasion, but today would be especially busy since she and her sisters had decided to move the seasonal inventory toward the front of the store where shoppers could easily browse. Not only would it be visually appealing, it would encourage sales. It did, however, mean clearing space on the shelves, something Elizabeth had volunteered to do before she realized how much work it entailed.

She set her cup on the counter with a small click and rolled up her sleeves. She'd tackle the chore one shelf at a time. Slow and steady. Like running a marathon or eating an elephant.

Laughing at the direction her thoughts had taken, Elizabeth scooped up a stack of dishes and moved them into a box on the floor. Not wanting the box to get too heavy, she added some tablecloths, a lace-fringed dish towel, and several homemade aprons before sliding it to one side to be moved to the back room.

A voice rose from the women gathered around the quilting table. "Rachel, is there any word on Moses Troyer?"

The name registered in Elizabeth's brain. Moses had a daughter named Emma who usually attended the quilting circle. She was absent today. Was someone in the family sick? Hopefully not, but along with pumpkin bread and Indian corn, fall also typically brought with it the start of cold and flu season.

Elizabeth's hands closed around a valuable crystal punch bowl and a set of silver ladles. "No box for you," she said, lifting the bowl gently off the shelf. She carried the bowl and ladles to the back of the store and deposited them safely onto a shelf. When she returned to the front she heard Rachel addressing the group.

"We are in agreement, then? Leora, you will organize a schedule for meals, and Marietta, you will do the same for housecleaning? It will be several weeks before Moses heals from his injuries."

All around her, heads bobbed in agreement, some covered with prayer kapps, others not.

Injuries?

The word played silently in Elizabeth's brain. She didn't know Moses Troyer had been injured. Wondering *how* occupied her thoughts while she packed the next three shelves.

At the front of the store, Elizabeth's sister Mary blew in on a breeze and a mechanical beep from the sliding doors. Martha followed behind, a basket of cinnamon-scented baked goods balanced on one hip.

"Wow, you've been busy." Martha nodded toward the empty shelves then hitched the basket high enough to slide onto the glass display cabinet. "We were only gone a little while. You got a lot done."

"Thanks, but I'm ready for a breather." Elizabeth ran her sleeve over her damp forehead. "Hey, did either of you hear about Moses Troyer being in some kind of accident?"

Martha pulled back the door of the display case and reached inside to make room for the new baked goods. "I didn't."

"Me neither," Mary said as she tied an apron around her waist. "Isn't that Emma Troyer's father? What happened?"

Elizabeth circled the display cabinet to help Martha. "Yes, that's him." She hefted the basket and moved it down to give Martha easier access. "I have no idea. Emma isn't at the quilting circle this morning. I just overheard Rachel and the others talking about ways they can help."

"Must have been a pretty serious accident," Martha said, putting the last loaf of banana nut bread in the display cabinet.

Mary checked her watch. "Maybe we could ask the quilters when they finish up."

Martha pushed the door closed and straightened. "I agree. If they're talking about helping the family, maybe there's something we could do."

Hearing them, Elizabeth's heart warmed. Before she could even ask, her sisters were considering ways they could help. Of course, that's how things worked in their little town of Bird-in-Hand. People cared for one another. It was one of the many reasons she loved living there.

"I'll make sure to ask Rachel before she leaves," Elizabeth said. Handing the empty basket to Martha, she nodded toward the next set of shelves with items to be moved. "If you need me, I'll be over there."

Elizabeth crossed to the shelf, where candlesticks, crockery, and an old electric clock stood side by side. Clearing the more delicate items took time, but eventually there was a space long and wide enough to accommodate several brightly colored pumpkins and a few fall wreaths.

Elizabeth had just placed the last item on the shelf—a vintage toolbox that had been converted into a table centerpiece—when the members of the quilting circle filed by. Some smiled at her and bobbed their heads in greeting. Others chatted about their plans for the Troyers, excitement making their voices bright. Rachel brought up the rear. Elizabeth reached for her elbow as she passed.

"Do you have a moment to talk?"

"Of course." Rachel waved to the members of the quilting circle and then moved out of the aisle next to Elizabeth. "The store looks lovely. You are doing a good job moving the fall decorations to the front where everyone can see the colors."

"Thank you, Rachel." Elizabeth motioned toward the chairs vacated by the quilting circle. "Did I overhear you say something about Moses Troyer being in an accident?"

Rachel's expression sobered. "Yes, that is right. His buggy was forced off the road late yesterday afternoon by a speeding car."

"Oh no." Elizabeth sucked in a breath. "Is Moses all right?"

"Thank *Gott*, he will be in time," Rachel said, nodding. "Besides some cuts and scrapes, he has a broken arm, and his ankle was fractured. It will be several weeks before he is allowed to put weight on it, but at least he is home now, resting."

"And what about the driver of the car?"

"As of this moment, we still do not know who was driving the car."

"You mean they didn't stop?" Elizabeth exclaimed.

Rachel shook her head, her brown eyes darkening.

Elizabeth's thoughts sped to Moses's daughter, Emma. Moses owned a dairy farm, which meant the work of tending to the animals would fall to Emma, since she and Moses lived alone.

"I'm glad he's okay," Elizabeth said, then sucked in a breath. Buggies often bore the brunt of accidents involving cars. "What about the horse?"

"Silas went by the Troyers' farm after he heard about the accident. He says the horse will be fine, just a few scratches. He will tend it while Moses heals."

Relieved by the answer, Elizabeth let out the breath. Too often, the result of such an accident was far different. "I heard you all discussing plans to help."

"*Ja.* Since Emma will be tied up with the farm, several of us will be taking meals to them during the week. And others will go by to help Emma with the housework and tending to Moses."

All of this sounded hopeful, but worried lines still furrowed Rachel's brow. "I am concerned about the farm though. I am going to stop by on my way home to see if Emma needs help with the cows."

Elizabeth's thoughts raced. Rachel's son owned a dairy farm. Would he be able to help? "Are you thinking of contacting Adam?"

"*Ja,* if Emma and Moses approve. I will speak to them first to see what they think."

Elizabeth glanced at the shelves she'd been working on and quickly made up her mind. Reorganizing the store could wait.

She tugged her apron strings loose. "Do you think Moses and Emma would mind if I go with you? Maybe there's something I can do."

Pleasure beamed from Rachel's face. "That would be *wunderbar.* I'm sure the Troyers would appreciate a visit." Her brows winged upward. "But the store?"

"Mary and Martha are both here. They won't mind, and they'll be glad we're looking after our neighbors," Elizabeth said. "Give me a moment to let them know where I'm going. Then I can drive us out to the Troyers'."

At Rachel's nod, Elizabeth folded her apron, stored it under the counter, then wandered the aisles in search of Mary and Martha. When she found them, Mary offered to finish moving the fall inventory, so Elizabeth happily made the drive with Rachel out to the Troyers' farm.

A long gravel drive split the pastureland in front of the Troyers' white farmhouse. Hemmed with fence posts and barbed wire, it wound like a ribbon past a large barn, worn gray with age, and two silos that towered over it like sentries. Here and there, black and white Holsteins polka-dotted the rolling hills, their bawling echoing off the line of trees that were just beginning to don their fall robes.

"There," Rachel said, pointing toward a spot near the door. "We will park and see if Moses is well enough for visitors."

Once they rolled to a stop, Rachel pushed open the car door, its dinging adding to the chorus created by the cows and one lone basset hound, whose low howl mustered fear in a murder of crows. They took flight as one, their glossy black wings stark against the leaves of a golden maple.

The screech of the screen door as Emma Troyer pushed through added the final note to the symphony. Elizabeth might have chuckled over it all had not worry and fatigue lined Emma's pretty face as she greeted them.

"We have come to check on your *daed*," Rachel said, "and see if there is anything we can do to help around the farm while he is laid up."

Emma's shoulders sagged beneath the pretty pink cotton of her plain dress. Her fingers sought the handle and then she pulled the screen door open again. "Daed is sleeping now, but please, come inside. I know he will be pleased that you thought of him." As they passed, she added, "I have a pot of coffee brewing. Would either of you like a cup?"

Rachel nodded, but Elizabeth held up her hand. "None for me, thanks. I've had my quota for today. Any more and I won't be able to sit still."

Emma led them past a sparsely furnished living room and down a narrow hall to the kitchen. Like most Amish homes, the wide room invited company and conversation. A sturdy table draped with a floral tablecloth dominated the center, and around it, six chairs waited to be occupied. Stirred by a breeze from the open window above the sink, a kerosene lamp suspended from the ceiling swayed, and against a cheery, robin's-egg-blue wall, a gas refrigerator hummed. It was from this Emma took a small pitcher of cream to set on the table next to a matching sugar bowl.

Rachel skirted the table to sit in the chair closest to the window. "So, tell us. How is Moses?" she asked in a quiet voice.

Taking her cue from Rachel, Elizabeth lowered her tone to match. "My sisters and I were very sorry to hear about your father's accident."

Emma's head dipped as she carried the coffeepot to the table. "*Danki.* He is mending, but the doctor says it will be some time before he is back on his feet."

Concern pulled at the corners of Rachel's mouth. "And that means more work for you."

Emma nodded, her knuckles white around the handle of the pot. "But we are making do. Daed has taught me everything there is to know about caring for the cows."

"That is as may be," Rachel agreed quietly while Emma poured her a cup. "Still, it is no chore to hold out a helping hand. Silas and the boys will be glad to pitch in whenever you need them."

Pride was something the Amish frowned upon, yet something akin to it was reflected in the angle of Emma's upturned chin. "Danki, Rachel. I will keep your offer in mind." She said the words carefully, firmly, then set the pot down with a thump that rattled the lid.

Her answer obviously did not please Rachel, whose lips thinned. Her gaze dropped toward the dark liquid swirling in her cup.

"Perhaps we can help out another way," Elizabeth offered, her words breaking the awkward silence that enveloped them.

Curiosity shone in the gazes Rachel and Emma turned to her.

Elizabeth leaned forward to rest her hands on the table. "I've never milked a cow before, but I'd be willing to learn."

Gratitude suffused Emma's face, and for a moment, Elizabeth thought she might accept, but then she smiled and shook her head.

"Danki, Elizabeth, but it's not the milking that troubles me. It is finding time to track down additional buyers. We have a few, but with prices being what they are, it has been harder and harder to break even."

Elizabeth chewed her lip as another idea struck. Most of the milk they bought came from Rachel's son, Adam, but Martha's baked goods sold well, so they could always use a little more. She looked at Rachel. "Do you think Adam would mind if we bought a few gallons of milk from Emma and her father while he is on the mend? Just to help out, I mean."

"Of course not," Rachel said.

Elizabeth turned her gaze to Emma. "It wouldn't be much, but it would be something."

"Having a new customer would be a big help, even if you cannot buy a lot of milk," she replied shyly.

"Good, then I'll talk it over with my sisters and let you know what we need."

"That would be wonderful, Elizabeth." Gratitude warmed Emma's voice. Her fingers shook as she reached up to smooth a wisp of hair that had escaped from her kapp. Poor thing. She was obviously more worried than she let on.

Throughout the exchange, Rachel sat quietly. Though she nodded when Elizabeth glanced her way, something in her gaze still whispered of concern.

Elizabeth wondered if the situation was more dire than Emma was letting on. Would the help they were offering be enough to get Moses and his daughter through this crisis?

A NOTE FROM THE EDITORS

We hope you enjoyed this volume of the Mysteries of Lancaster County series, created by the Books and Inspirational Media Division of Guideposts. We are a nonprofit organization that touches millions of lives every day through products and services that inspire, encourage, help you grow in your faith, and celebrate God's love in every aspect of your daily life.

Thank you for making a difference with your purchase of this book, which helps fund our many outreach programs to military personnel, prisons, hospitals, nursing homes, and educational institutions. To learn more, visit GuidepostsFoundation.org.

We also maintain many useful and uplifting online resources. Visit Guideposts.org to read true stories of hope and inspiration, access OurPrayer network, sign up for free news-letters, download free e-books, join our Facebook community, and follow our stimulating blogs.

To learn about other Guideposts publications, including the bestselling devotional *Daily Guideposts*, go to ShopGuideposts .org, call (800) 932-2145, or write to Guideposts, PO Box 5815, Harlan, Iowa 51593.

Find more inspiring fiction in these best-loved Guideposts series!

Secrets of Wayfarers Inn
Fall back in history with three retired schoolteachers who find themselves owners of an old warehouse-turned-inn that is filled with hidden passages, buried secrets and stunning surprises that will set them on a course to puzzling mysteries from the Underground Railroad.

Sugarcreek Amish Mysteries
Be intrigued by the suspense and joyful "aha" moments in these delightful stories. Each book in the series brings together two women of vastly different backgrounds and traditions, who realize there's much more to the "simple life" than meets the eye.

Mysteries of Martha's Vineyard
Come to the shores of this quaint and historic island and dig into a cozy mystery. When a recent widow inherits a lighthouse just off the coast of Massachusetts, she finds exciting adventures, new friends, and renewed hope.

Patchwork Mysteries
Discover that life's little mysteries often have a common thread in a series where every novel contains an intriguing mystery centered around a quilt located in a beautiful New England town.

Mysteries of Silver Peak
Escape to the historic mining town of Silver Peak, Colorado, and discover how one woman's love of antiques helps her solve mysteries buried deep in the town's checkered past.

**To learn more about these books,
visit Guideposts.org/Shop**

Sign up for the
Guideposts Fiction Newsletter
and stay up to date on the books you love!

You'll get sneak peeks of new releases, recommendations from other Guideposts readers, and special offers just for you . . .

and it's FREE!

Just go to Guideposts.org/Newsletters today to sign up.

Guideposts®

Visit Guideposts.org/Shop
or call (800) 932-2145